SCRAPS & CHUM

Published by: Grand Mal Press, Forestdale, MA

www.grandmalpress.com

Scraps & Chum Expanded, Ryan C. Thomas, copyright 2016
Library of Congress Cataloging-in
Publication Data
Grand Mal Press
p. cm
Cover art by Grand Mal Press

Spoiled Meat: (Originally published in Undead: Flesh Feast 2, *Permuted Press)*

Siren (Previoulsy unpublished)

The Pinch (Previoulsy unpublished)

Bleeding on the Rug (Originally published in the novel Sam, *by Iain Rob Wright)*

Squeaky Wheels (Previously unpublished)

Cookies Have No Souls (Originally published in Space Squid #3)

The Runner and the Beast (Previously unpublished)

One of These Days (Previously unpublished)

Martin's Job (Previously unpublished)

To Protect and Sissonne (Originally publisheshed in Nanobison, vol 3, issue 7)

Brothers Til The End (Previously unpublished)

The Hallowed Shortcut (Originally Published in Hallow's Eve: An Anthology to benefit READ)

Ginsu Gary (Originally Published in Splatter Punk #3)

SCRAPS & CHUM

A COLLECTION OF SHORT STORIES

BY RYAN C. THOMAS

GRAND MAL

P R E S S

TABLE OF CONTENTS

INTRODUCTION..9

SPOILED MEAT...13

SIREN..28

THE PINCH...45

BLEEDING ON THE RUG...............................64

SQUEAKY WHEELS...80

COOKIES HAVE NO SOULS...........................111

THE RUNNER AND THE BEAST....................114

ONE OF THESE DAYS.....................................152

MARTIN'S JOB..160

TO PROTECT AND SISSONNE.......................176

BROTHERS TIL THE END..............................183

THE HALLOWED SHORTCUT.......................193

GINSU GARY..209

INTRODUCTION
by Craig Saunders

Let's talk about horror a while, shall we? Unrelentingly dark, violent, sickening, challenging . . .

What? That doesn't sound like fun at all. Ryan's not one of those writers. I'm glad about that, because I wouldn't have fancied reading this collection in the slightest. I know he's not all about darkness. I've been a fan of Ryan's stories for several years now. Sure, they are dark, and probably violent and gory and sick in places (my standards are probably somewhat different to those who like *Sailor Moon* and Sandra Bullock movies, mind you), but those things I can live with . . . it's horror, after all. It's not supposed to be about soul searching in the midst of a love triangle with the gardener on top, but about the actual insides of people, and what's inside isn't just viscera and the squishy bits. It's hopes, dreams, thoughts, feelings. The pie competition in "The Body" (or the movie *Stand by Me* if you prefer), or many of King's earlier short stories—these are dark tales, but sometimes funny, and overall entirely human. There is something gleeful about the fiction here and humanity is the star, and humans are just as mean as the monsters sometimes . . . but we love, too, and make mistakes, and go to the toilet accidentally when we've had too much to drink. That kind of golden horror era always worked best for me, and writers like the aforementioned King, Robert McCammon . . . they still work. Because they understand people. Even in the belly of the beast, or that alien overlord's muctile maw, people still crack inappropriate jokes.

Of course, horror's a catch all term— it's speculative fiction without quite as much cuddling and a little bit more blood. Perhaps while cuddling. There are conventions, yes, like in most genre fiction, but it's not the conventions of the genre that draw me in, nor the setting (I do like a nice bit of horror in the snow, and zombies I find cute and adorable). "Squeaky Wheels" meets those conventions, but then it's almost British in the humour, reminiscent of Hutson or Herbert. Ryan does creature features with a little sprinkling of the absurd on top. Or tales like "The Runner and the Beast", where Ryan stretches his creative legs, or "Siren", where you feel his disappointment through the protagonists eyes . . . or maybe it's just the protagonist's and it's only fiction. Thing is, it's real and cinematic and it puts you right there where you lose yourself and the author and that's a great thing, isn't it? Good fiction makes you forget you're reading at all.

There's a sense I get reading Ryan's work that he's enjoying himself as he writes these tales, and that impression's formed right from the first story in this collection, "Spoiled Meat", when we watch the main character feed undead people as though they were pigeons in a park. His writing's visual, descriptive, visceral. He paints a picture and it's a personable kind of fiction, accessible, and it sucks you in. Like you're watching small movies, these short stories; *Creepshow, Tales from the Unexpected*, maybe—eeeew . . . but with a smile.

I've known Ryan a while and he's an aficionado of the bizarre, the ridiculous, the insane. He published my work, we talk, we work together. Because how can you not dig a man who likes Douglas Adams? Here's a collection of shorts that remind me of that grinning joy at finding a short story full of wicked grins and a wink from the writer; Kurt Vonnegut taking a stroll down a poorly-lit back lane in *Welcome to the Monkey House*; Roald Dahl's darker moments in *Kiss Kiss*; King, in *Skeleton Crew*.

I enjoyed the hell out of this and like "The Pinch" . . . it's contagious.

Craig Saunders
The Shed
2015

SPOILED MEAT

YESTERDAY IN THE park, I fed the zombies, tossing bits of cadaver flesh onto the cold cement as they fought each other like pigeons for the morsels. They're not so different from pigeons, really, when you think about it, driven as they are by a primal need to feed, to sustain.

The pigeons, by the way, are all gone. I ain't seen a four-legged creature in some time. Not even a dead one. They're all just . . . gone.

Anyway, yesterday, one of them creatures that was feeding, a small girl of about seven or eight, still in pigtails, ate right from my hand, licked the blood off my fingers and moaned for more. That was a first for me, and I thought it was a good sign. I kept urging her to bite, saying, "come on, just a nip, you can do it, Precious." But she didn't. Frustrated, I drove my hand into her top teeth and drew blood from the veins on the back of my hand. But nothing happened; no sickness overcame me, nor did it get her chewing on my goods. I held my hand out longer and longer until she licked it clean like my Labrador used to do to my dishes after some spaghetti, but she still wouldn't bite. And just like a dog—to keep this analogy chugging forward—she sniffed around my chest and legs, looking for meat I might have hidden. But I had no more to feed her.

Clean meat is scarce; uninfected corpses have been hard to come by lately. I know there's one under a car near the bookstore. The zombies have been trying to get him for a couple days now, but he's wedged under there good, his head all sunken and his belly distended. Died from hunger, that poor guy did. Hell of a way to go, right? Perhaps tomorrow I'll dig him out and cut him up . . . if I can get him back to my "home" before the zombies tear him limb from limb. The zombies. The Zees as I call 'em now . . . just to break up the boredom.

Maybe I could tie the chunks of meat to me and see if that works, see if they take me in the process.

Where was I?

The little girl. Yeah, the little girl, eyeball dangling on her cheek like a cat toy, she finally gave up and went foraging. But the others, they stood around me just waiting, eyeballing me hard, as if I could pull fresh meat from the air and fill their bellies. "Don't you look at me like that," I yelled. "I got the freshest meat this side of hell. Look," I said, holding up my hand so they could see the bite mark from the girl's teeth. "Look at it. Smell it. It ain't bad. Taste it! For Christ's sake just try it!" But they didn't listen, just stood there swaying, looking up into the sky, maybe waiting for it to rain. Oh they can hear, don't get me wrong, they got ears like boom mics, but if it ain't alive—aside from me any-way—they don't give a shit. I looked at my hand, my knuckles pruned from the little girl's tongue, and started to cry.

Tears make the time go by these days.

When the sun went down I made my way over to

the 7-Eleven for some fine dining. All around me, the Zees shuffled about, moaning and groaning like the Mormon Tabernacle Choir played at 33 rpm. I used to complain about the noise from my neighbor's stereo, that Satan music, big metal or angry metal or whatever they call it, but what I wouldn't give to hear it now, to hear something different than these things bellyaching all damn day and night.

The 7-Eleven's power has been out since I got here, and half of the store is burned to the ground. The canned food aisle made it through pretty much untouched, though, and so I grabbed a can of Chef Boyardee and opened it with the can opener I keep in my pocket. Room temperature, but God, food is food, right?

I cried while I ate, that much I remember, sitting there, tears rolling down my face, a Zee staring at its reflection in one of the cooler door windows. Mixed in my tears with the imitation raviolis and swallowed it all down.

When I was done, I tossed the can at the Zee to see what reaction I could get. Damn thing didn't move, didn't even notice a can just bounced off its head.

The gun in my pocket called out to me again, like it did every day. Like Romeo to Juliet, in a metaphorical sense, you know. It begged to be used.

But I can't do it. If I take that route . . . I'm dead. I mean really dead. Gone. Nothing. I don't want to be dead . . . I want to be undead. I want to feel something, even if it's just aching hunger pangs and a yearning for brains. I don't want to stop feeling.

Ain't that what life really is? Feeling?

And so I sat and cried some more—tick tock tick tock—and eventually just fell asleep on a candy rack covered in melted chocolate bars.

• • •

When I awoke this morning in the 7-Eleven, a group of Zees was looking down on me, their drool landing on my chest and soaking through to my skin. How best to describe the odor of Zee drool? You ever—whoever you are, who finds this dog-earned notebook one day—you ever open a trashcan that a baby's diaper has been festering in for a couple days, all out in the sun and stuff? Now cover that diaper in fresh puke from the town drunk . . . okay, you get the idea. It's like that. Better than any alarm clock when it comes to getting you out of bed, that's for sure.

"Morning, sunshines," I said. This was met with a witty retort, or what I guess would be a witty retort if I could speak zombie. To me it sounded like one of them didgeridoo things from Australia.

They said the plague was a global problem—what'd they call it, a pandemic?—before all the radios and TVs went dead. But I bet there are some bush people in the Outback that survived. Well, maybe. Maybe not. It's been a while. And it means shit anyway because where the hell would I get a plane or ship to get there. It's been . . . what . . . six months now . . . and I ain't seen a living soul. I've driven/biked/walked from Dallas to San Diego, and bupkis.

I rolled off the Hershey's mattress and looked outside, saw it was another beautiful day for being the most unwanted man in existence.

Getting over to the bookstore was a huge pain the ass, what with the cars all flipped about and the Zees all following me around waiting to be fed, tripping me up like cats running between my legs. Like I got a chef's hat on or something. They know I can get the food.

They can learn, the bastards.

Once I'm gone, I want to keep on learning as well. I want to be a part of something.

There was a time maybe I didn't, when I wanted nothing but peace and quiet, and was happy to hole up in the TV room downstairs. Got to the point most people said they didn't want me around anyway if I was gonna be like that—which reminds me of the time Brandy asked me what ostrich sized meant—and I think at first I was sorta happy 'bout the prospect of a Zee plague. But now . . .

As I walked, I started thinking on that whole situation, remembering what it was like in the school basement. Boy, that was dumb hiding down there, with no real way out and nothing to eat but big cans of unsalted corn and beans meant for the school cafeteria.

Someone, one of the town folk I'd never seen before, had a radio, and we'd been listening to static that morning, being as how the airwaves had been dead for over a week. The Zees were scratching at the door, shaking it, making it rumble in the jamb. They'd been doing it for longer than the airwaves had been dead, so we'd kind of gotten used to it. Ain't that pathetic? The radio, however, was pissing me off something fierce.

"Can't you turn that shit off?" I said. "Ain't no one gonna broadcast nothing."

"Some of us are still optimistic," the man with the radio said. "You should try having some hope."

"And you should go chat with what's on the other side of that door. Give all of us some more room to move. Take that damn radio with you."

"You really are a jerk, Mr. You know that?"

"I know lots, like you're heating up my nerves. Them things out there want you, they better hope they get in before I beat you dead with that radio first."

I was contemplating taking a swing at this guy when the door swung open. Don't ask me how . . . must have been all that yanking and pushing and pulling for two weeks straight, and the damn thing just gave. Them creatures were piled so high on the other side they literally spilled into the room, grabbing at the nearest piece of flesh they could see. The screaming was deafening as everybody ran around all helter skelter, taken by surprise, swinging pots and pans and yardsticks. I punched, I kicked, I shoved hard, the blood in my ears cutting out the sound of people being eaten alive all around me. In the confusion, the ground came up to me right quick, Zee feet stepping on me as they went after their quarry, and so I called it quits and lay there waiting for my turn. Tick tock tick tock.

Want to know the crazy part? I fell asleep. Yup, right there in the middle of all that carnage, waiting for my turn, I fell asleep. I'd heard of guys doing that in the war, some kind of defense mechanism of sorts. What's crazier, of course, is that I woke up again.

Untouched.

When I got up, some of my former compatriots were shuffling around, having joined the enemy so to speak. All around me, the Zees paced back and forth, ambling around with blood on their lips, flesh stuck in their teeth. Thing is, the basement door had shut again and some bodies were in front of it, acting as a big doorstop. The Zees were scratching on it, from the inside now, just like dogs. Yeah, like dogs, remember? I got up real slow, waiting for them to notice me, waiting for the inevitable to happen, not really sure why I was still alive anyhow. Not caring about much neither.

"Hey," I said to the room, "you missed me. Come on, get it over with." I opened my arms in a hug.

They looked at me, looked back at the door, went on pacing.

They didn't want me.

Sheeit, I thought, now ain't that just a bit off kilter. Why didn't they want me? Didn't make no sense, you know? They shoulda been all over me, pulling my meat from my bones like I was a Thanksgiving turkey. But they couldn't care less. What they really wanted, I learned after some time—time spent staring straight ahead, fighting to rationalize my position in all of this—what they really wanted was for me to open the damn door. Because when I finally pushed through them, grabbed a bulk size can of corn off one of the shelves (most of the shelves were tipped over, the cans all ruptured when the others had used them as weapons) kicked the bodies outta the way and opened the door, they immediately made for the hallway beyond it, and eventually, the door to outside.

On the street in front of the school, I sat on the curb and watched all the Zees walking around on the sidewalks, on the lawns of nearby homes, down the center of the roads. They all passed by me and gave a look my way, maybe stopped and stared for a few seconds, but none came over. Hell, I even took to throwing rocks at them to see if I could get their attention, but they's a one-track-mind kind of species I learned.

The sky was black with smoke from a thousand fires burning all over the county. I didn't hear no birds singing or dogs barking or cats howling. It was just me and the Zees.

At first I didn't know what to feel, but by nightfall, it started to sink in that I was really alone. Not the kind of alone I'd wanted before, where I could turn on the TV and see a ballgame, or get a hello from Jack at the liquor store, or stare at that single mom two houses down who wore them tight pants. I mean really alone. Unwanted. Ostrich sized.

Two streets over was the Episcopal church, so I got up, grabbed my can of corn again, and made my way over to it. The door was open, the stained glass shattered, and there were Zees inside, which seemed a bit disrespectful to me, them being in God's house and all. But then, who's to say all this mess wasn't God's idea, some sort of cleaning method so he can start over fresh.

I pulled up a pew and stared up at Jesus on the crucifix above the altar. "I don't get it," I said. "Everybody's gone, all eaten and come back as something else. But not me. There something I'm missing here?"

No reply. Nothing.

And then I cried, which was the first time since Korea I'd done that. It was a real cry too, the kind you just can't stop once it starts, the kind that goes on until you're dry inside, the kind you gotta fight to breathe through. Some time later, I looked at Jesus again and begged him to take me too. "I'm lonely," I said. "I don't want to die. Everybody else, they get to keep on going, even if it's as a monster. At least they got something. At least they got each other. You're leaving me with nothing. Nothing! Tell me what I did!"

The can of corn knocked the cross to the ground.

I fell asleep in the pew.

● ● ●

Where was I . . .

. . . tangents, tick tock, tears . . .

Oh yeah, this morning at the bookstore.

The area outside the bookstore had its usual collection of hungry monsters hobbling around it. I'd given some of them names, the ones I'd seen around a lot: Goopy and Scabby and No-Arms and Pussface. When they saw me coming, saw the other Zees following me like puppies, they ambled my way as well, as if to say, Thank God, can you please help up with this big metal doohickey, our ball rolled under it and we can't get it.

"Yeah yeah," I said, pushing through their numbers as they sniffed me and played with my shirt (I think they could smell the last bits of good meat I'd tossed out). "I see your food, you dumb idgits. I'll get it for ya. But first, anybody want an appetizer?" I held up my arm, took out the can opener and ran the dull blade across my forearm. As the blood began to trickle out, a few of them stepped forward and inspected it, but just like the other times I'd tried this, they lost interest and went back to moaning at the car.

Throwing my head back, I screamed at the heaven's "What! What the fuck did I do! Why not me?"

Of course, there was no answer, same as that day in the church. Well, I think one of the Zees farted. Which, really, about summed up what God was doing to me anyway.

"I ain't doing it myself!" I shouted again, just for good measure, pulling out the gun and waving it all crazy-like. "I ain't ending it like that. If you want me, you take me like you took the rest! This ain't fair!"

And I sat down and started boo-hooing again, which lately, had become my shtick. "What's wrong with me, what's wrong with me, what's wrong . . . " Over and over and over, rocking like a Weeble.

At some point I felt one of the Zees push me, like to say, hey buddy, get to it already. Goopy and Pussface were standing next to him, anxious for me to get up as well. Like I said, just like dogs.

"All right, back off," I said, standing up and going over to the car. Past the car in the window of the bookstore was a paperback I'd thought about going in and getting a few times now. Maybe today I would. Maybe it was time to get out of this town—I could use the reading material for traveling. Maybe I should leave tomorrow. The roads are still pretty jammed up with crashed cars and ambling Zees, and I can't ride a motorcycle to save my life, but the bike shop nearby has some good selections. Maybe Mexico would fare better for me. Maybe I could even keep riding down to Panama or something.

Dropping to my belly, I reached underneath the car and grabbed hold of the dead man's pant leg. His head was all jammed up in the pipes, his eyes still open and dry as chalk, and I had to pull pretty hard to get him out. 'Course, once his leg hit the sunlight those Zees pushed me outta the way and went to town, big time.

Hoping against hope, I thrust my arm into the feeding frenzy and felt one take a nibble on my pinky. Hurt like a bitch, but it felt so damn good to be wanted. But the sonofabitch pushed my arm outta the way like it was broccoli on a plate of chocolate cake. Fuckers didn't want me after all. Same old same old.

Yanking some carnage from No-Arm's mouth—in case I needed some for later—I went into the bookstore and grabbed the paperback in the window. It was *The Painted Bird* by Jerzy Kozinski. I'd read it ages ago, and it depressed the shit outta me, but right now, I needed to know someone else felt my pain. Needed to know that someone else out there, even if he was fictional, was as unwanted as me. Rolling it up, I stuffed it in my jacket pocket, made my way back around the Zees, who were all on their knees ripping every last bit of flesh and sinew off that rotted cadaver, and headed back to the park.

The pigtail girl was there again, just sitting on the bench, cradling an unopened can of Coke like it was a baby doll. Let me tell you, when you have no one to talk to, the walls become a real good audience. These Zees were no different than walls, and so I sat down beside her and looked in her eye, the good one that wasn't swishing about on her cheek, and struck up a conversation.

"Hi, Precious," I said. "What you got there? That your baby? What's its name?"

If it had been a real baby it woulda been an unhappy one because she tossed it on the ground and growled at it as if it had ruined her life. Satisfied with that, she took up sniffing my coat again and discovered the meat I had in my pocket. Suddenly ravenous, she started to tear into the leather, her strength much greater that you'd expect, so I turned away from her and got my hand on the meat before she rendered me naked. Judging by the look of it, it was a head scrap: an ear and part of a scalp, some hair stuck to it on one end. When she saw it she lunged at me.

"Hang on, hang on, Jesus you guys don't know shit about patience, do ya?"

So I wrapped it around my fingers because, you know, I had to keep trying, right? Had to hope one of these times the bite would work for me.

And you know what she did, as I gave her my hand and said, "Here comes the plane, into the hanger." Know what she did? She unwrapped it! Took it off my hand and wolfed it down and didn't touch me at all.

"Oh, come on!" I shouted. There was no way she was getting off that easy, so I grabbed her head and opened her mouth and stuck my nose in it and pushed her jaws closed until white light erupted behind my eyes and blood ran down my throat. Did that for about ten seconds until I realized I wasn't going to do shit but lose a nose and have to walk around sounding like a teakettle as the wind blew through the new hole in my face.

Needless to say I gave up.

Afterwards she sat there, blood streaked on her cheek, her dangling eyeball starting to droop a bit lower, and just kind of looked at me.

"Brandy," I said, calling her by my granddaughter's name—it just came out of nowhere. She didn't look like Brandy, who'd had blonde hair and freckles before she died, didn't look like her at all, save for the age part. "I miss you."

And then it just came out, outta nowhere, outta that part of my head where important things get buried: "I shouldn't never have yelled at you that day." She, it, whatever, made a sort of cooing sound and dribbled some blood onto the bench and I chuckled a little bit, which was a good feeling. "I shouldn't never have hit you neither, young as you were. Not for that anyway. Not for breaking a watch I hardly wore anymore. Fact is, I shoulda laughed at your ingenuity, cooking it in that pot of stew like that. Pretty funny now. Certainly shouldn't have smacked you in the face for it. I get angry, you know, just can't help it. I . . . I'm . . . Maybe I can make it up to you? Maybe we can go—"

Before it went any further though, she got up, shuffled over to the Coke can, picked it up carefully like it was a crystal vase or something, and walked away into the shadows.

Leaving me alone. Again. With tears. Tick tock. Tick tock.

And so here I am, sitting under the moonlight in a forgotten park, writing to you—whoever you are, who finds this dog-eared notebook—getting ready to head south. The world's most unwanted man. Me. Tomorrow morning, way I see it, I'll grab some Chef Boyardee and get going on down the I-5. Maybe the Mexican Zees got a better bite.

Can't help but keep thinking—hold on . . . this teenage one's licking my neck . . . please please please . . . Shit! No dice. He's leaving now . . . back to wherever he goes at night I guess.

Can't help but keep thinking about what my wife said a few weeks before all this began, before she died and came back and ate our granddaughter. She said I was dead inside, that my heart was nothing but a ball of mud, all stinky like skunk cabbage. We didn't get along so great those last years, always fighting and cussing and ignoring each other. And, well, shit, I don't know you—whoever finds this—so I'll just admit that I hit her too. A few times. Great, now I'm getting these words all wet.

Yeah, I hit her. Hard, more than a few times actually. I get angry, you know.

And she said all my bitterness and anger killed any sense of humanity I had.

I told her I didn't care, and went to my TV room downstairs and just stayed there, alone, and didn't come out for . . . well . . . until those reports started about the dead people.

I bet she's staggering around back there in Dallas, laughing inside that bloody husk she got as a body now. I bet she's laughing hard as I used to hit her.

No Humanity left.

Maybe she's right.

Because here I am.

SIREN

THE FIRST MORNING I heard it, I thought I had left the television on overnight. You know, that extremely high-pitched whine, almost on the edge of hearing, yet audible on some peripheral plane. The sound of an electrical component silently sucking juice from an outlet. I wiped the jeweled crust from my eyes and reprimanded myself; I could not afford to be so negligent these days. Electricity cost money and my wallet was thin, especially with gas prices so high and me having been let go by the school. I rolled over in bed and saw the empty bottle of Black Label tipped sideways on the floor. Had I finished the whole damn thing last night? I didn't even remember making it to the bedroom.

The whining sound did not sit well with the heat peppering the backs of my eyes. Whiskey dries me out, gives me pimples to boot, but mostly makes my eyeballs flame up. Problem is once I start drinking it I don't stop.

I rolled out of bed, intent on finding the source of the whine. When I was a little boy, a friend of mine had a dog whistle that emitted a similar tone. He'd blow it and nearby mongrels would howl and look at us longingly before barking and finally whimpering, begging us to stop the torture. This was the sound I heard that first morning, as I threw back the blankets and stared at the blue sky outside the window. It persisted as I held my head and stepped over the pile of clothes on the floor and ambled to the living room.

"Ow," I said to whatever ghosts might reside in my home, and hit the power button on the cable box. I was walking toward the bathroom when I realized I could still hear it. "Ugh." I returned and hit the power button on the television this time. The TV turned on, an annoying talk show, so I shrugged and turned it off again. I headed once again to the bathroom, convincing myself the distant high-pitched wail in my ears was actually just my head playing tricks on me.

You're hung over, take a shower and you'll feel better.

I did regain a semblance of humanity as the hot water beat into the back of my neck, the pulsing behind my eyes slowly disappearing. I let the water pound my face and head, and drank big gulps of it as well, hoping it would hydrate me.

Thoughts of the previous night's writing session came back to me. The story I had been working on was still unfinished, and I was clueless as to where it was going. It seemed I'd been writing some version of it for years, though I only had twenty pages to show for it. The story was boring, unimaginative, and stagnant. That I was able to get the twenty pages out of it was a pathetic moral victory. I had not been able to write anything of merit in some time, and my last novel had gotten less than stellar reviews. A review in one of the more notable literary magazines said it felt like McGovern (that's me) had employed a new method of writing while lobotomized.

It's hard to teach English to high school students when they know you're a joke. Even harder to keep teaching it when you tell them they'll never amount to anything. The district frowns on such truth.

After the shower, I dressed myself and sat at my computer, looking over what I had written the night before. It was pitiful, so I sighed and deleted the entire thing. "I've read better shit on bathroom walls. Read better stuff by that Davidson kid."

I dwelled on Davidson. One of my former students who had sold his first story to a magazine I'd been rejected by repeatedly. It was infuriating; the kid couldn't spell his own name. But editors stopped caring about prose long ago; nowadays they just want tropes that sell.

I tell myself that anyway.

Frustrated, I went to the kitchen and rifled through the cabinets until I found what I was looking for: a bottle of aspirin and some Bagel Bites. I put the coffee pot on and rifled through yesterday's mail. Nothing but bills I couldn't pay now that I'd been fired.

That was when I realized I could still hear the hitch-pitched whine in my ears.

II

Over the course of the next day I convinced myself not to go on a bender. I wrote a little, hated it all, deleted it, and then watched bad talk shows. The whine remained. And what's more, it got louder. I checked every electrical component in my apartment but could find no source for the sound. By the second day the whine was making me irritable and I felt like those dogs from my youth, shaking my head to rid myself of the annoyance, sticking my fingers in my ears for a brief reprieve. Unfortunately, my fingers did nothing to block it out.

On the third day, the sound was too loud, simply grating, and I gave up trying to write or understand the slang and memes on the talk shows, and walked down the road to O'Connor's Pub. The sound followed me like a loyal dog, slowly and steadily getting louder, like car brakes squealing across town. I glanced up at the power lines and transformers as I made my way to the pub, but could find nothing that might betray its origin.

It was inside the pub that I first realized something was truly amiss. Several patrons were pressing their fingers into their ears. I took a tattered stool at the bar and motioned Pat O'Connor over to me.

"Hey there, McGovern," the Dubliner said. "Been a while since I've seen you. Working hard or hardly working?" As he spoke he gave his head a slight shake, an obvious testament to the uncomfortable effects of the sound that was somewhere in the air.

"Pat," I said, glancing around the pub, "do you hear that noise?"

"Does the pope shit in the woods? Yeah, been hearing it for a couple of days now. Damndest thing. Any ideas?"

"Not a clue. But I'm glad I'm not going crazy."

"I think it's the power lines," he suggested. "Or that new complex down the street . . . they got that free internet set-up. Uses all them cables and whatnot. That's probably what it is. Damn annoying. I'm gonna call the electric company if it don't stop soon, give them a piece of my mind."

"Yeah," I replied, knowing full well that such connections did not create irritable resonances.

A pair of twenty-somethings walked in, wearing jeans three sizes too big and t-shirts with marijuana leaves on them. They sat next to me at the bar and one of them waved for Pat's attention.

"Muthafucka!" the bleached-blond one said, "Yo, Pat, you got the windows open or sumptin. You gotta shut 'em. My ears are killing me, yo."

Pat told the kid that the windows were all closed.

The kid's friend, an angry-looking man with a shaved head and sideburns that met under his nose, slammed his fist on the bar. "Fuck, man, this shizzle is givin' me a straight-up headache. I can't hear myself think or nuthin'."

Blondy pretended to swat a fly for emphasis. "For rizzle, my nizzle."

My ears, hurting though they already were, seemed to throb a bit more at such poor English. I was unaware that I was staring at them until the blond addressed me.

"What up, Pop? I look funny to you or something?" He turned to his bald friend, said, "Yo, dog, check this muthafucka out. Like he's mesmerized by my beauty an' shit."

"Straight up, Bee. Pops thinks you a shorty or sumptin."

I felt like I was back in my classroom just last week, listening to the devolution of language by the same primates who would someday be wiping my ass in an old folks home. As an author and teacher who had devoted his life to the written word it disgusted me to hear such ignorant speech. Don't get me wrong, I'm all about colloquialisms and fun slang. I remember saying Far Out and Groovy and confusing my father until he just shook his head at me. The last ten years teaching high school English gave me the ability to interpret teenage nonsense, but the way these idiots talked sounded like someone had injected a virus into the nature of coherent communication. As I listened to these two youths, who probably spelled "ask" by rearranging the last two letters, I couldn't help but fear for the art I loved so dearly. It was bad enough all these horror and sci fi authors were making the bestseller lists, with their penchants for gore and sex and robots—-such drivel—but to think one day there might be novels published in such incoherent nonsense made me want to leap off the nearest cliff.

"Sorry," I said, and ordered a whiskey from Pat. I drank it down and left.

III

The weekend passed, a meaningless couple of days to a newly jobless man such as myself. The high-pitched sound rose steadily and I now found myself getting a headache, eating Tylenol as if they were Tic Tacs and stuffing cotton balls in my ears. I finally called the electric company and tried to get some answers. They had a prerecorded message saying they were aware of the problem and were trying to solve it.

I sat in front of my computer, desperately trying to ignore the noise and complete chapters to a novel I'd started years ago. Again, though, my writer's block kept me from turning out anything meaningful, so I turned the computer off and stared at my kitchen cupboards. I was out of chips. I was also out of booze. I am not a drunk, despite what you might think. The other night's drinking session was a capricious incident, an attempt to find a muse and forget recently being made redundant. And visiting O'Connor's just gives me something to do now and then. But I did consider the notion that perhaps some alcohol would help me deal with the grating noise.

"Welcome to the Bank of Desperation," I said as I dug through couch cushions looking for dimes and quarters. As I treasure-hunted, I listened to the television, which was now showing news reports concerning the strange whine that seemed to be everywhere. Nobody had yet been able to find its source. The phone companies were also reiterating, rather angrily at this point, that they had no idea where the sound was coming from. The news flashed B-roll as the story unfolded. The entire town was wearing earplugs.

"Sound specialists and geologists from several Universities are running tests," the reporter said, "but have not concluded anything significant yet. We also have confirmation that the sound is being reported in other cities, both domestic and international. Officials are assuring people they will find its cause very soon."

Captions scrolled across the bottom of the screen as the man talked. He too, was wearing earplugs. I noticed they used the word ORAL when they meant AURAL. Idiots.

As I walked to the store the sound level jumped up emphatically. It made the backs of my eyeballs twitch in pain.

The store was suddenly full of people racing about in a panic. Like birds at a feeder, they fought one another for the remaining stock of bread and milk. I laughed at the notion that such items would serve any purpose at the end of the day. Everywhere I turned, people were holding their ears and asking each other what the noise could be. Babies were crying, and the store was cacophonous with their collective wails. I grabbed two bottles of Jim Beam and paid for them in the checkout line. Beyond me, a young mother in her early twenties was yelling at her child. "Oh please, Chelsea, just shut yo mouth. Damn, girl, I can't deal. There ain't nothing I can do about it. For real."

I took my liquor and shuffled outside as quickly as

I could, once again sad for our dwindling sense of elo-
quence. Was I really that much of an elitist, I wondered. Some people did not have access to an
education such as I'd had. Should I blame them for
being raised with that type of vernacular? Still, I could-
n't help but fear that perhaps the reason my books
weren't selling was because people weren't reading anymore. My students had thought a gerund was a small
animal, and took greater pains in learning what rhymed
with the N word so they could be hip hop stars when
they failed out of school. I felt like the butt of a joke,
like the subject of dramatic irony. Everyone around me
knew our precious written language was dying out,
evolving into senseless code, and they embraced it; I
still believed I could utilize its dying breath to secure
my future. What a joke.

On the way back home, eyes squinted and fingers
in my ears, I passed by a park. Some children ran in a
circle and threw a rubber ball at one another while an
older woman in a long blue coat watched them intently.
A young boy threw the ball at a young girl and hit her
in the face. The girl fell down crying, and the woman
rushed over and picked her up. She grabbed the boy,
and made several wild gestures at him. The boy responded in kind, and I realized that he was deaf, that
it was a class of deaf children. I can't read sign language, but I could tell some sort of heated argument
took place next among all the students. Hands maneuvered quickly, fingers dancing and wrists twisting, con-
veying thoughts I could only guess at. I stared

fascinated for a few minutes, ignoring the grating sound in the air, thinking what a hard life it must be to not hear. Then remembered I was carrying my booze. As I turned toward home, I noticed that none of them were wearing earplugs.

IV

By morning the sound was unbearable. If I closed my eyes I envisioned someone standing right next to me scraping a fork on a ceramic plate. My neighbors began congregating in the street, staring at the sky and shaking their heads. A few of them wore earmuffs, while others had hats pulled over their ears. Surprisingly, no dogs or cats seemed to be in any discomfort. The pug nestled in my neighbor's panicked arms was as happy and excited as he was any other day.

I had given up on writing or looking for a new job and focused solely on alleviating my ever present headache; even with my earplugs in and my mind succumbed to the alcohol, the sound was too intense to ignore. It seemed to radiate from thin air, which explained the people in the street staring at the sky. Only by getting drunk had I been able to ignore the noise and fall asleep the previous night, but when I woke up it was right there again, everywhere and nowhere at once. Incredibly piercing. I felt lucky to have gotten the little sleep I did. The black circles under my neighbors' eyes told me they were not so lucky.

"Time to get the hell out of Dodge." I looked for my car keys, trying to decide between heading to my parents' house up North or going out West to the beaches. Then I remembered the news and realized I might not be able to get away from this maddening sound.

The television was still reporting on the phenomenon on every channel, tired reporters pointing toward space and shaking their heads. Images from the Middle East and Africa and every other place imaginable showed similar scenes of confused and terrified people yelling at the sky. Everybody on Earth seemed to be experiencing the same thing.

It was evident the electric company had nothing to do with it now. Experts from the world's top research centers were meeting with the world's leaders, or so the news reported. At some point during the day, someone had drawn up a sign and placed it on the side of the road near my home. It read: THE END IS HERE BEOTCHES!

I became scared.

I had no idea where I'd put my keys.

V

Oh my fucking God! Unbearable!

The sound suddenly soared to such an unearthly high decibel level around noon that small cracks stitched down my window panes. The walls vibrated. I pressed my hands over my earplugs and ground my teeth, sweating and swearing. It was all I could do to maintain rational thought. An hour later the world's leaders declared a state of emergency. How they had the strength to make decisions was incredible. The news reporters, in some mockery of standing in a soundwave hurricane, winced in pain and shook their heads as they reported, barley getting words out. All flights were stopped, schools were closed and kids were sent home, work ceased, the National Guard rolled in to watch the State House, the nation's military scattered around D.C., FEMA mobilized in every major city. It did no good; no one could withstand the noise. Everyone was useless. Car accidents were clogging up the roads. Lunatics were firing off guns.

I was sitting at my computer marveling at the terrifying news online, fingers in my ears, teeth clenched as the whine—now a raging siren—raked my mind, when I noticed one of my neighbors in the street fall over.

So loud and so high-pitched was the noise at that point, a thousand fingernails scraping a thousand chalkboards would not have come close to the agonizing frequency it put forth. My hairs stood on end and my eyes watered. I could not focus for too long on any one thing before the screaming siren sent my vision wobbling.

And then, it rose again.

"Jesus Christ," I shouted as I stumbled to my window, "it's killing me! Oh, God, make it stop! What's happening!"

My eardrums shrieked with pain. My temples threatened to tear open. I ran around my house, looking for a way to stop the pain, banging my head on the walls. "God, please!" Outside in the street, pandemonium had set in, and people ran fruitlessly in circles, hands over their ears, teeth grinding. Army trucks sped by, helicopters flew over the horizon.

Peering out my front window, I watched as the people in the street stumbled and fell. Blood burst from their ears, running down their necks and shoulders. I could see them screaming but I could not hear them. In the distance, a car swerved into a tree and its occupant spilled into the road like dirty laundry. He rolled around holding his head, his hands stained bright red. Those who had remained in their homes came running outside, blood spitting from their ears onto the ground, long trails of red forming behind them, turning the street into some bad abstract painting.

My brain felt like it was being stabbed with screwdrivers, the pressure in my head swelling until I thought my eyes would shoot out of the sockets and run down the window pane. Still the sound rose in pitch and intensity.

All of us now. Dogs. Howling. Begging for a reprieve.

"Dear, God!" I pleaded repeatedly, as if a man who had shunned the church eons ago would suddenly get a personalized letter from the Almighty. Of course not; my yelling and wailing went unheard even to me. "Oh my God! Make it stop!"

Outside people writhed on the ground. The sun began to set.

Finally, the window exploded.

And something in my head popped.

I felt hot, sticky liquid running down my fingers. Pulling my hands away from my ears, I saw blood flowing down my wrists and dripping onto the carpet. I grabbed the nearest whiskey bottle and drank until it was empty. At some point I landed face first on the floor. Waves of nausea rolled over me before I finally passed out.

VI

When I woke up, there was no more pain. People were walking in the streets, helping one another up. Everyone's ears were coated in blood.

I have been scared of many things in life, most notably my own failure. My first novel was well received in the underground market, my second not so much, and the third largely ignored. I had spent many years with writing groups. I read as much classic literature as I could. I disciplined myself to turn out only the most quality narratives I could create. At every turn, the nation instead emptied its pockets for stories that were written for a dollar, not an aesthetic. What was worse, I had thought I could spread my love of the written word to my students, only to be thwarted at every turn by a technological revolution that twisted language into an abomination of inhuman laziness; I wanted to scream the day I graded my first paper written in Leet.

When the world went deaf, I found myself with renewed hope that literature, once again, would take precedent as the most popular form of entertainment. What good was a sitcom or an action film without sound? How interesting was a rock and roll band that couldn't be heard?

While people ran in the streets, bleeding from their ears, crying and banging pots beside their heads, while society's dregs slipped in and out of homes and businesses, taking advantage of this new opportunity to move undetected and steal whatever they wanted, and while religious zealots everywhere sacrificed goats and cats to a new angry God that wanted us to suffer eternal silence, I turned back to my stories. For weeks, I ignored the madness outside my window, and wrote all day and all night, some of the best material I have ever produced.

This was all a few months ago.

The world has resumed a sense of normalcy, if you can call the myriad sign language classes at every church, school, and community center normal. The ground's bloodstains were washed away with weeks of street cleaning. There was a mad dash for televisions that offered closed-captioning, and the latest films are shipped with subtitles. These are priorities.

The nightly news subtitles are garish, accurately transcribing slang and expletives, spelling "ask" with the last two letters reversed. I understand the romantic use of portraying society as it is, but I fear. I fear for a generation growing up reading such nonsense. I fear for the children who will learn this as their language.

I fear we've been given a chance to once again embrace true art, true language as the Renaissance poets meant it to be, and we're snubbing it.

My books and stories still do not sell and I don't know how to teach sign language because I am still learning it myself. I am going broke. As are many.

I wince at the store, as I buy my whiskey, and see people passing notes to each other, tiny communiqués rife with abbreviations: What u do 2nite? How R U doin? Call L8R. I have made it a game to guess what they are saying, what the real words used to be. Sometimes I figure it out, sometimes I'm baffled. Always I'm annoyed.

As I walk by the park on the way home, I watch the deaf children, those original deaf children, play ball and flash signs to each other. Their hands are graceful and swift, bobbing and flexing with fluidity, each finger a tiny ballerina. I see them roll their eyes at strangers, the newly deaf, who destroy their art form by creating their own, more vulgar, variations of the language. I feel for the children.

Their art is being bastardized.

The source of the sound was never discovered. For all we know, it is louder and shriller than ever before. Not one single human on Earth can hear anymore. But sound still exists. The animals will come if you call them. Just the human race was punished. No one has an answer why. I suspect . . . because we took advantage of our gift.

I sit at my computer, continuing to write, hoping someone will read this or anything else I've labored over, hoping I can revive the art of our written word. As I type I watch the captions on the television scroll by. They are misspelled, full of slang I do not understand, and mixed with numbers and symbols that supposedly make them easier and faster to read by a world of morons.

I have no idea what they're talking about.

I am in Hell.

THE PINCH

NICKY WAS WALKING out of the candy store with his best buddies, Greg and Willy, when a little boy with an eyepatch ran up and pinched him on the arm.

"Son of a—" shouted Nicky, rubbing his flesh, jerking away from the strange boy. He watched as the skin on his bicep turned pink before his eyes. "What did you do that for, jerk?"

The little boy, a few years younger than Nicky and his friends, stood alone on the street, his messy hair blowing about like a miniature wheat field. He laughed the way little boys do when they don't understand they've just done something wrong. Probably he had seen it on a cartoon or in a comic book, thought Nicky, and was imitating some character. Greg had a little brother who always did annoying things like that, which was why they never included him in their activities.

Nicky contemplated hitting the boy, at least shoving him, but knew that if his mother heard he was in a fight he'd be in a world of trouble. After all, he wasn't even supposed to be at the candy store; it was on the main road and he was forbidden to ride his bike past the end of his residential street. If she knew he'd punched some kid on the main road, he'd be grounded for sure. And being grounded during the summer was a real bummer.

The flesh on his arm began to itch, and a bead of blood formed on the wound. For a little kid, thought

Nicky, he sure pinches hard.

From the salon next to the candy store a bug-eyed woman appeared and grabbed the little boy's arm, yanked him away. For some reason Nicky couldn't decipher, she wouldn't look the boy in the face as she yelled at him, just kept her eyes on the ground, as if she were scolding his feet. "There you are! How many times do I have to tell you not to wander off! You made Mommy worry!"

"The little brat pinched me," Nicky said, presenting his arm for her inspection. Behind him, Willy and Greg sucked in their breath, amazed at his impudence.

The woman leered at the three boys, a frown spreading across her face, her head shaking as if it was *them* that were bothering her son, and yanked the boy down the sidewalk to a parked SUV. She hurriedly strapped him in the backseat and got behind the wheel, glancing sidelong at Nicky's arm and whispering, "No." The kind of *no* not said in annoyance, but said to affirm that what she was seeing was simply not true.

Which meant nothing to Nicky and his buddies.

The boys watched the woman through the SUV's window as she fumbled the keys in her lap, snatched them up, and jammed them into the ignition. A tear ran down her cheek as the vehicle pulled away from the curb and drove off. In the rear window, the little boy rudely stuck his tongue out, and Nicky could have sworn the boy's one good eye was red.

Dark red, he thought, like it was filled with blood.

"What the hell was her problem?" Willy asked,

shoving a Milk Dud into his mouth.

The SUV turned at the intersection, taking the corner fast enough to make the tires squeal, and was gone.

Nicky looked at his arm once again, saw the wound had swollen to a light purple bump, felt the itchiness intensify. It reminded him of last summer, when he got poison ivy playing in the empty lot at the top of his street where the old gas station had been torn down. Yet this was just a tiny mark, hardly something that should bother him as much as it was. Scratching it, he discovered, only made it worse.

"Did you see his eye patch?" Greg asked.

"Yeah, I wonder what happened," Willy responded. "You think he only has one eye, like maybe he was born without it?"

"Or maybe he poked it out somehow," Greg said. "My Mom said that her friend poked her eye out running with scissors. The eye rolled near the dog dish and the dog ate it."

There was a collective "Eewwww!"

"Aw, that can't be true," said Nicky, still rubbing the welt. "She's just trying to scare you. Like when she told you not to make faces because you'd stay that way, and you were afraid to stick your tongue out when the doctor wanted to check your tonsils."

"It really happened. I swear!"

"No it didn't."

"Yeah it did!"

"Did not!"

"Come on," Willy said. "Let's get home before *Star*

Trek starts. It's the one where Q tries to kill Piccard."

"Q always tries to kill Piccard," Greg said, rolling his eyes. "What's new about that?"

They jumped on their BMX bikes like cowboys mounting stallions, and crossed the main road at the intersection, heading toward Sunders Lane and Nicky's house. They each made sure to jump the same sidewalk cracks and spit at Ms. Hutchinson's mailbox—she lived on the corner of Sunders and never gave out Halloween candy. At the vacant lot that used to be the gas station, they jumped the bike ramp they'd made earlier in the day—-a piece of plywood angled up onto a cinderblock.

With each pump of his feet, Nicky felt the bruise on his arm growing larger, hotter, itchier. He scratched it repeatedly as he pedaled, a couple times even taking both hands off the handlebars. Could it be infected? God knew what crud the brat had touched that day. And then he remembered the eye. The one reddish eye. Was it really red, he wondered, or was I seeing things, a trick of sunlight through the window?

They skidded into Nicky's driveway, gravel spitting into the air, dropped their bikes on the grass and raced to the front door. Together they went to the rumpus room downstairs to watch *Star Trek* and satisfy their sweettooths before they had to disband for dinner.

Nicky kept rubbing the welt.

● ● ●

At dinner, he told his parents he'd been stung by a bee. The mark on his arm was now a full-blown red and purple wound, like a bright strawberry birthmark. If he didn't know better he'd swear he'd been bitten by some kind of large, venomous bug. When he touched it, it felt soft, like a rotten peach. But the few beads of blood that had formed on top had faded away into a tiny scab.

"Stop itching it," his mother told him, "and go wash it off before you get it infected."

"Mom, I don't feel—" Vomit shot out of his body with such force he pulled a muscle in his neck.

"Jesus, Nicky!" Helping him to the toilet, his mother rubbed his back as he expelled his dinner. When he was done he flushed, closed the lid, and sat on the toilet rubbing his arm.

"You don't look good, Nicky," his mother cooed to him. "That thing looks like it might be genuinely infected. You've never been allergic to bees before. You're burning up, though." As she spoke she inspected the wound, twisting his arm to see it in the light. "It doesn't look like a bee sting."

"Mom?"

"Yes, Nickums?" She only called him Nickums when he was sick. It had been his baby nickname.

"I lied. I went to Candy Mountain. That's where I got the bite. Only it's not a bite. A stupid boy pinched me."

"You went to the store? Dammit, Nicky—"

"I'm sorry, Mom."

"How many times have I told you—"

"I know, but I had that five bucks from Nana...and anyway a boy with an eyepatch . . . "

His mother gave him a look that said she'd discuss his punishment later, but that right now she was too concerned about his arm. "Don't know any boys with eyepatches," she said. "But if I ever see him I'm gonna give both him and his mother a lecture on hygiene. You probably got yourself an infection from his dirty hands.

"Well, swab it with Peroxide and hop in bed and we'll see if it's any better in the morning. I'll call the doctor when I wake up and see if he can squeeze you in. I hope you realize I have to take time out of work now because you disobeyed my wishes. You may have the summer off but I have to work. I have to make money so you can have all the nice things you want, like bikes to break my rules with."

Nicky hung his head. The nausea had passed, but his arm still burned and itched, and on top of that, he felt guilty for disrespecting his mother. "I'm sorry," he said.

He shuffled out of the bathroom, instinctively picking at the scab on the wound.

"Don't pick it," his mother shouted. "That'll only make it worse. Get in bed and don't pick it."

•   •   •

Nicky lay in bed, a cold compress on his arm that his mother had given him after cleaning up the bathroom.

Staring at the ceiling, he thought about the boy with the eyepatch, saw his face in the granulations of paint. Dirt marred the boy's forehead and cheeks like leopard spots, some type of sticky juice or candy was crusted at the corners of his mouth, he wore a shirt with a Pokemon character on it, light blue shorts stained with what looked like grape jelly, and green Velcro sneakers. The eyepatch was not a toy; it was made of heavy leather and had a curved inner edge to fit around the boy's nose, clearly made by medical professionals.

As Nicky stared at the illusion above him, he remembered the force of the pinch, stronger than a boy that age should be able to muster. Pain had been instantaneous, like someone burning him with a match. The tiny fingernails had clipped the skin, drawing blood before Nicky even had time to react. Fast and hard and sharp.

And the boy's mother . . . had she been leering at him because she thought he was bothering her boy? Or was it something more? The more Nicky thought about it, the more it seemed she'd been afraid. But why? Did she know what her son had done? Was she ashamed? Why hadn't she just spanked the brat, or at least scolded him?

Sleep came like a rainstorm, lightly at first, but soon powerful and overwhelming. But dreams of firecrackers and new bikes were constantly interrupted by vignettes of the boy with the eyepatch: the boy's one good eye pulsing red, lobster-claw hands that snipped at his sides and back, sending bits of flesh to the ground like confetti. In the dream, Nicky wrestled with the boy, rolling in ribbons of his own skin, until finally he punched the boy in the stomach and sat on top of him.

"Gimmie this patch," he said. Without hesitation, he yanked it off, and fell back screaming. From the boy's black socket poured forth a collection of moans and a stench so foul it rivaled the time he found the decomposed raccoon under the oil drum at the vacant lot. Accompanying the moans, gray and rotted fingers thrust out from the socket, groping and flexing like giant worms wriggling for freedom. They cracked the ocular bones as they forced their way through the hole, reaching out toward Nicky. Hands and arms followed, the boy's skull crumbling as something hideous tore loose from inside, the moaning growing louder and louder! Something black and vaguely human tore its way out!

Nicky woke up sweating.

● ● ●

It was the kind of morning that foretold a scorcher of a day. Outside, birds were singing and the neighbor's dog was critiquing it. Down the street a lawnmower was growling a familiar summer tune.

Nicky rolled out of bed and wiped the sleep from his eyes and made his way downstairs where he found a box of Cheerios already waiting for him on the table. The note next to it said his mother would be home early from work today to take him to the doctor.

Cheerios weren't nearly sweet enough for his taste buds but his mother forbid all the fun cereals like Cocoa Puffs and Apple Jacks, so he added sugar from the sugar bowl. As he sat eating, he rolled up his sleeve and looked at his arm.

Black!

All Black!

The spoon hit the floor and catapulted milk toward the ceiling as Nicky jumped up from the chair. His entire bicep was covered in a large black scab. "What the hell . . . ?" he whispered.

Brrring

He ran to the phone, picked up the receiver. "Mom, you have to come home—"

"Hey sweetie, need me to change your diaper?" There was a guffaw. It was Greg.

"Oh, it's you."

"Don't sound so excited."

"Listen, Greg, something happened to me. My arm . . . it's . . . it's . . . "

"Missing? Morphed into a penis? What?"

"Where that kid pinched me, it's all gross."

"Gross how?"

"I dunno, just gross. Black and scabby, like sandpaper." He traced his finger across it, felt the crispness of the skin.

"Maybe you've got spiders growing under your arm. My mom once said a close friend of hers—"

"Jesus, Greg, shut up! I'm serious. Look, I have to

call my ma, I'll call you back."

Greg's voice was cut off as Nicky pressed the button to clear the line. He called his Mother's office. Mrs. Dewberry, the receptionist, answered in her perpetually cheery voice. "Hi, Nicky," she said. "Your mom ran out with the boss for a quick meeting. She said if you called to tell you to stay home till she gets there. I heard you had a run in with some thug yesterday. Everything okay?"

Thug? Jeez, he thought, the kid was younger than he was. But then, he couldn't proudly tell Mrs. Dewberry he was bested by a grade-schooler. The thought made him so angry he wished he could bike over to the boy's house and punch him in the face. Only he didn't know where they boy lived. All he knew was that the boy's mother got her hair cut at . . . Wait a minute, he thought, the hairdresser might have the woman's address. And if he could find out where the boy lived he could find out what had been done to him.

"Nicky? You there?"

"Yeah, Mrs. Dewberry, yeah, I'm fine. Um . . . I'll just see her when she comes home. Bye."

He hung up and dialed Greg back. "Greg's Pizza Parlor, would you like to try our special dingleberry lover's pie?"

"Greg, get Willy and meet me at my place in ten minutes. We're going to Candy Mountain."

"Again? I don't think I can eat any more Twizzlers. My piss was purple last night."

"I want to talk to that salon next door, see if they

know anything about that kid."

"What about your arm?"

Nicky looked at his arm, which looked like a hamburger that had been left on a grill too long, and felt his anger growing hotter. "My mom is taking me to the doctor at noon. That gives us three hours to get some answers. Hurry up."

He hung up the phone. As he ran up the stairs to change into jeans and a T-shirt, he noticed that the black scab had moved down past his elbow.

It's spreading, he realized. And a new sense of horror flooded him.

• • •

The three boys pedaled with all their might, racing against time, not even stopping to spit at Mrs. Hutchinson's mailbox or jump the ramp at the vacant lot. None of them sat down, standing and pumping their legs furiously as they tore down to the candy store. Each bunny-hopped up onto the curb, simultaneously launching themselves off the bikes mere inches from the salon's door. It was closed.

"Shit!" Nicky yelled, banging his fist on the door.

Greg and Willy gaped at Nicky's arm, which they'd been doing since meeting at Nicky's house. "I think it's getting bigger," Willy said. He stuck a finger out to touch it but pulled back.

"Now what?" Greg asked.

"I suppose we could ride around and check out the

side streets," Nicky said, "maybe we can find the SUV."

"That could take days," Willy said.

"Shit," Greg reiterated.

All three of them banged on the door in anger.

"We're closed already!" came a voice from inside.

"Holy crap," Nicky said, "someone's here."

All three shouted. "Let us in!" "Open up!" "Now!"

A tiny woman in jeans and a yellow blouse opened the door and stood blocking the entrance. Her hair was frosted three different colors. A mug of coffee was in her hand.

"We ain't open yet. And you rugrats can't get a haircut without your parents anyway."

Nicky spoke up. "Please, we just need to know about the boy with the eyepatch."

"What the hell you talking about? I'm cleaning up. Come back later."

"No," Nicky said, placing his foot between the door and the jamb. "Look what he did to my arm."

"Jesus, kid. You should go to the hospital."

"The boy with the eyepatch did it. I don't know what's going on, but it's getting worse. Who is he?"

"Eyepatch?"

"Listen, lady," Greg said, growing frustrated and unafraid to show it, "if we don't find this kid, Nicky is gonna end up an amputee."

Nicky's eyes bulged; he hadn't even though of that.

"No, you listen, kid, I don't give out client information."

Threats were not Nicky's strong suit, but he decided to play the card anyway. "If you don't tell me I'll cut my own hair and tell my mom you did it."

The hairdresser sipped her coffee. Age and fatigue were visible on her face, and perhaps it was sheer apathy, but she chose not to argue. "Nice try, kid. Even a bad cut by me is a good cut."

"Please, lady. Look at my arm. Please. At least if we know what the kid was touching we can tell the doctor."

She sighed, puckered her lips as she took in Nicky's arm. "Sheeeit. All right, yeah, the kid with the eyepatch. I don't know his name. His mother comes here about every six months to get a cut. You know, funny you should bring her up, she usually gets the same cut, but this time she got it cut shorter and had me dye it blonde. Not a good look for her, believe me. She don't talk, you know. I try to ask her things, what she's been up to, how her kid is, that kind of stuff, but she don't talk. Keeps her kid in the car, never brings him in. He sits back there with a comic book but I figure, hell, he looks well fed, seems happy. I don't know. I saw her grab him yesterday, so I guess he got out. I think she's embarrassed by him, the whole missing eye thing. Strange that she went blonde, you know. I don't know what else to tell you."

"Where do they live?" Nicky asked.

"Look," the woman said, "I give you this woman's address and you cause her problems, and she sues me or something, I'm gonna find you. I see you down here at the candy store so I know you're from around here—"

"We won't tell," Nicky said. "Please. My arm is going numb."

"Hang on." She disappeared inside, returned a minute later. "Lucky for you I have a mailing list she signed up for. For coupons and stuff. She lives up on Roseland Drive. It's by the supermarket. Name's Tara French" She handed Nicky a Post-it with an address. "Now get out of here. And go see a doctor."

The door slammed shut.

● ● ●

Roseland was a cul de sac two blocks away from the market, full of ranch style homes with big lawns and two car garages. On the front lawn of one house some children were kicking a soccer ball—though none of them was the boy with the eyepatch.

Winded from the ride, the three boys dropped their bikes on the sidewalk and walked up to the front door of Tara French's house, across from where the children were playing. Nicky blew on his arm; the sun was making it itch again.

"I hope that brat answers so I can pop him," Greg said.

Nicky rang the doorbell. No one answered. They rang again. Nothing.

"They moved," came a voice from the street. The boys spun around and found a small girl standing at the edge of the lawn holding the soccer ball. "They moved last night," she said. "I watched them from my window. They were making all this noise I couldn't sleep. They had big bags and suitcases. What's wrong with your arm? It's all gross. Are you moving in there?"

Across the street, the girl's mother popped her head out the front door and called her back. "Gotta go," the girl said, and ran across the street, back to her yard where she threw the ball at one of the other small children. The little girl's mother glared at Nicky and his buddies, waiting to see if they were up to no good.

"She's spying on us," Willy said, "let's warp outta here."

"Shut up, Willy," Greg replied. "Look at Nicky's arm. It's almost down to his hand."

The black scab was spreading down Nicky's forearm, reaching toward his wrist, as well as spreading around the back of his bicep up toward his neck. He bent it and winced as the scab split in the crook of his elbow, releasing yellow pus and blood.

"That is fucking-A disgusting," Greg said.

Nicky studied the window next to the door. "Maybe we can get in here."

"What for?"

"To find out where they moved to."

Thunk!

The sound came from inside.

Greg plastered his face to the window and peered between the gap in the curtains. "Holy shit. Something is in there."

"Lemme see."

All three boys squinted through the window. Inside, a fully furnished living room was bathed in shadow, and through an archway off to one side a kitchen table was just visible. A foot stuck out from under it, twitched for a moment and then went still again.

"Quick," Nicky said, "around back. Someone's in the kitchen."

Willy started to debate but Greg grabbed him by the shirt and yanked him around the back of the house. Once there, Nicky tried the back door, which swung open with a fart-like creak. Willy shook his head in silent protest, his breathing heavy, but Greg glared at him and pointed at Nicky's arm and that was that. Filled with trepidation, the boys entered.

The kitchen was dark, the shades drawn. Against one wall a green refrigerator hummed, a drawing done in crayon hanging on it with a magnet. Dishes were scattered on the floor, trash was overflowing from a large white garbage can, the scent of rotting meat hung heavy in the air, flies buzzed everywhere.

"Man, it stinks like crud in here," Greg said, holding his nose.

Willy's hand went to his mouth as he slowly backed up against the door. "The table. Look," he said.

Under the table, a black mound rolled about. Like cheap balled-up saran wrap, it slowly unfolded and grew larger into something humanoid. Just like what came out of the boy's eye in my dream, Nicky thought. As they watched in horror, it opened its eyes and reached a hand out toward them——a black hand, crusted and covered in yellow pus and blood. It spoke: "Go 'way."

It was a man, or man-shaped anyway, no longer doubled over but clearly in pain, propped up against the baseboard.

"Go away," it breathed again.

The boys remained frozen, terrified and mesmerized.

"Get . . . out . . . now"

"Who are you?" Nicky asked, his legs shaking.

"Get . . . out . . . "

"Fuck this," Willy said, "I'm outta here." He tore through the door.

Fighting his paralysis, Nicky approached the black thing under the table. It breathed heavily, as if trying to speak, as if forming words was taking every ounce of its energy.

"Um . . . Nick . . . " Greg was backpedaling toward the door now, too.

Nicky bent down and ran a finger across the black scab that was the man's face. In fact, the whole body was one giant black scab. Nicky held up his arm, comparing his scab to the man-thing on the floor. "He pinched me. Did he pinch you?"

The man looked at Nicky's scab, closed his eyes and sighed.

"Nick, I don't like this." Greg was half out the door.

"Hang on." Then, to the man: "He pinched me too. What is it? How do you stop it?"

The human scab slithered out toward the center of the floor, the dried skin crunching and cracking like

Pop Rocks. In the shadows, the whites of his eyes were about the only things visible. Greg stepped completely out the door, his knees vibrating.

"Wife and I," the man droned, rigid once again, sucking in labored breath, "tried for years. Drugs . . . herbs . . . whatever bullshit theories were . . . in news, we tried it. But couldn't . . . get pregnant. Figured . . . what the hell, pray to God . . . ask him for help. But . . . no answer."

Blood was running down the man's hard, cracked skin. Greg couldn't look at him, but Nicky bent down closer.

"Can't blame me," the man continued. "Can't—too young understand anyway. God wouldn't . . . give us child. Our future. So . . . who . . . what was left? Devil ain't real. Devil . . . is for comic books . . . movies. But . . . I asked, and nine months later. No eye . . . but swore to love him. No eye . . . should have seen it. Just skin . . . smelled bad. No eye...no soul. Could tell."

"Please," Nicky said, "How do you fix it? Wake up."

"Look at me! You think . . . I'd be like this . . . if I knew how stop it. He was . . . such good boy until . . . sixth birthday. Then stopped talking. Phases, they said. But no. Phase is when . . . wife stops fucking you . . . when you go to church again. He pinched . . . the dog. We took it to vet . . . couldn't do anything. Died big black scab. Disintegrated . . . black ash. And even when he pinched me . . . I thought . . . dog must have got disease . . . because . . . boys can't do such things. Look at me! I've been . . . inside house for . . . weeks. Doctor's couldn't figure out . . . even specialists. Left hospital . . . couldn't help me. Sit here rotting. Wife left . . . took the boy. Doesn't believe me . . . he's evil. No eye . . . but always sees you. Always finds you. Wife . . . doesn't . . . believe . . . Thinks I chase her . . . hurt boy. She . . . right. Evil. Devil heard me, heard my prayers. He's real. He—"

Tears rolled down the man's scabby cheeks as his breath gave out. And like that, he was dead. The tips of his fingers fell away into a pile of ash on the floor, scattered in the breeze coming through the doorway.

"Nicky," Greg said, "is he . . . ?"

"I think so."

"We gotta go get help, it's almost noon."

Nicky backed up slowly through the door, stepped into the yard with Greg. He held up his hand in the sunlight. It was all black. As was the side of his neck. Lifting his shirt, he touched the black scab that was working its way down his ribs. Try as he might to speak, he couldn't find the words. Breathing was beginning to hurt. Something inside his body felt like it was hardening. The pain was slowly taking over.

"Nick," Greg asked, "what's the hell's going on? It's all over you."

Tears cut from the corners of Nicky's eyes, just like they'd done from the dead man in the kitchen.

Willy was beside Greg now, watching Nicky cry, watching as the boy stared in disbelief at his own body. They stood there for a long time as a cloud of black ash blew out from the kitchen door.

BLEEDING ON THE RUG

"HE'S BLEEDING ON the rug, on the rug on the rug . . . "

Two days of lifting heavy boxes for the move to the new house had sucked the ever-loving life out of Dane. He should have been able to sleep through an elephant stampede. But the sound of Matti's frantic whispering shocked him out of his dream like a hooked fish yanked from a pond. There was something about his wife's voice that had the power to weave through his fatigues and mental blocks and grasp him.

" . . . bleeding on the rug on the rug . . . "

Sleeptalking was not uncommon for Matti; it was in fact a trait of hers Dane found endearing. On several occasions over the years he'd listened with a smile as she conversed with the denizens of her dream worlds. Sometimes a conversation with him, sometimes a chat with friends, sometimes just pure nonsense that made him giggle. But from the sound of her voice now, she was engaged in a nightmare. He decided he would give her a reassuring squeeze and tell her she was just dreaming.

" . . . on the rug, on the rug . . . "

"Roll over." He rubbed her side

Shadows hung heavy in front of him as his eyes struggled to adjust to the darkness of the bedroom. The clock beside the bed threw sanguine light onto the nightstand in the form of digital numbers. One rule

Dane had while sleeping was to never look at the time; counting the hours until work always gave him anxiety.

Too late. He saw it was 3:45 and compulsively did the math until he had to get up.

"Matti," he grumbled again.

". . . bleeding on the rug on the rug on the rug . . ."

His wife lay on her back, auburn hair in waves across her face, not a typical sleeping position for her. She was a fetal sleeper, often cradling one of the many teddy bears Dane had given her on birthdays and anniversaries. This position looked too rigid, almost forced, like she'd been tied to a board. And there was something about the way she was repeating the words that didn't feel right. Her voice was hushed, the words fast and sharp, like she was trying to say it as many times as she could in under a minute.

"Honey, wake up, you're dreaming." He grabbed her upper arm and gave it a little shake. Usually, this method resulted in angry instructions not to wake her up for no good reason. He'd recount the episode to her in the morning, like he always did, and she'd tell him he was crazy and out to sabotage her sleep. Such was their little joke.

But she didn't stir as he touched her, just kept on repeating the sentence, which was beginning to creep Dane out. Who in her dream was bleeding on the rug?

"Honey, you're having a nightmare. C'mon, roll over."

"He's bleeding on the rug bleeding on the rug . . ."

He shook her again, this time harder, hoping some

subliminal part of her mind would sense it and she'd at least roll over angrily.

Still, Matti didn't respond to his commanding nudge, which shook the hair from her face.

With his mind inherently doing math problems—three hours until I get up, I'll never get back to sleep at this rate—Dane gave it a second while his eyes adjusted. Finally, her face swam into view.

He gasped.

Her eyes were open, staring up at the ceiling. Her skin, pasty white, shined with sweat.

The muscles in his body snapped to attention and he sat upright, a reserve of energy suddenly powering him. What the . . . ?

Her mouth moved quickly as she spoke, like a mouse chewing on a bread crumb: "He's bleeding on the rug, on the rug on the rug . . . "

"Matti, what's going on? Talk to me. Matti? Matti?"

Letting her go for a moment, he leaned over and turned on the bedside lamp. The room jumped to life, the shadows retreating in the wake of navy blue curtains, a pale green comforter, lilac walls, and boxes of clothes and accessories that sat in piles near the closet, ready for the morning's move. She did not respond to the light, remaining consistent in her rapid decree that someone was bleeding on the rug.

Urgency welled up in his chest; he grabbed her head and shook it, said, "You're freaking me out. Wake up! Baby, c'mon!"

"He's bleeding on the rug on the rug on the rug . . . "

Eyes still open. Staring through Dane as if he were made of glass.

A cold, crippling sense of helplessness rendered him immobile. What the hell was going on? Was it a seizure? Did she need medical attention? Oh God, please don't let something be wrong, he thought. Not his wife. He'd have to be committed if something happened to her. The depth of his co-dependence came from left field and hit him hard. It was more than the feeling one gets when they lose something they never knew they had. He *knew* what he had in Matti; he just never figured he *could* lose it. Now he was flooded with doubt, and the frailty of life and love and marriage became something tangible, something breakable. Despite the fights and bickering, he loved her on a level too complicated to explain. She was simply a part that completed him, and here she was in a state of duress, scaring the living shit out of him.

Your wife is having a breakdown, Dane. She's non-responsive. Just pick up the phone and dial 911. Yes, he thought, that's something he could do, that was a plan, a way to break the iron grip of fear that now held him.

There was a phone on the small desk near the wardrobe. Throwing the covers off of his feet, he rushed to it and dialed 911. When he realized the only sound he could hear was the persistent voice of his wife, he figured he'd misdialed. He hung up and tried again. This time, he could tell the phone wasn't working. The phone company was set to turn off service in two days; had they jumped the gun? But 911 was supposed to be accessible regardless of account status. He slammed the headset back in the carriage and swore.

"He's bleeding on the rug on the rug . . . ." Matti was still on her back, still looking up at something only she could see.

Try the phone in the kitchen, he told himself. Hurry.

The hallway was dark and crowded with packing materials but he didn't waste time with the lights; he knew this house by heart. Knew that just yesterday he and Matti had made love on the top stair to break the stress of boxing up their belongings. A pang of sentimentality hit him as he descended the steps and maneuvered between the boxes at the bottom, realizing he'd be leaving this place come morning. He and Matti had lived here since before they were married, had even held their intimate reception in the backyard. How inappropriate that he should be thinking of this as she lay upstairs in some type of mental breakdown. Was it a survival instinct, he wondered, a way for his brain to keep him focused on something?

He rounded the corner into the kitchen, saw the phone as a black shadow on the wall near the cabinets, and grabbed it. Apparently the dead line upstairs wasn't an isolated incident; either the phone lines were down or someone had cut the wires outside the house. But then, that couldn't be right, because there was a noise coming from the phone after all. A hissing static, faint but definitely there. And beyond it, at the edge of audibility, a woman's voice saying, "help me, he's bleeding on the rug, he's bleeding on the rug . . . "

"Hello?"

The faint voice came again through the phone, came from somewhere far away, urgent and fast: "help me, he's bleeding on the rug . . . "

The phone dropped from his hand, swung on the tangled cord and banged into the wall, swishing back and forth like his own senility. Out of the earpiece continued the now familiar susurration, growing louder: "He's bleeding on the rug . . . "

Matti's voice drifted down the stairs and oozed into the shadows, providing a complementary backing vocal to the refrain: " . . . bleeding on the rug . . . "

It was confusion that he felt first, not terror. An innate need to rationalize what he was experiencing. And so he stood in the darkness of the kitchen, more boxes around him, listening to both voices chant about the blood on the rug, asking himself just what in the hell was going on? There's always a logical explanation for strange events, he knew. Looking around, though, all he could see was a nearly-empty kitchen. There weren't any answers jumping out at him. *Figure it out later. Right now you need to call for help.*

Cell phone, he thought, where was his cell phone? He'd been packing up books in the living room before going to bed and was pretty sure it was in his jacket on the table. Was it still charged, he wondered, or should he just cut across the lawn to his neighbor's house and wake them up, tell them to call an ambulance and maybe even some men in white coats?

No, he couldn't leave Matti, not yet anyway. He could feel that in his gut, that need to protect her, that need to make sure she was okay. For her sake, of course, but also for his. Because if anything were to happen to her . . .

As he passed the front door, moving through the foyer that separated the kitchen from the living room, he saw the Dust Buster sitting on a taped-up box and picked it up. He didn't know why exactly, it just felt right. Having some kind of weapon in his hand gave him a sense of advantage, even if it was a false one, and led him to believe he could still keep control of the situation.

That is, until he stepped into the living room and saw the figure standing near the sofa, bleeding on the rug.

Dane froze, his heart kicking into overdrive as his body went slick with sweat and his tongue dried up into cardboard.

The lanky figure was shrouded by shadows, its shoulders hunched forward with poor posture, its hair wispy and short. Judging by the lack of effeminate curves, it was a man. Whoever he was he was holding a hand to his head, his body swaying ever so slightly, as if a light breeze might blow him over. There was something decrepit about him, but at the same time . . . strangely formidable.

He's here to hurt Matti, Dane thought. Have to protect Matti.

The table in question was off to his right, equal distance from both him and the other man. His jacket lay in a heap on top of it, his cell phone in the front pocket. If he tried to run for it, and the man lunged after him, they'd meet at the same time. Dane hadn't been in a fight since high school, wasn't even sure he remembered how to defend himself? Still, he knew he'd fight for Matti, come what may.

Using the Dust Buster to mimic a gun, his heart now trying to rip through his chest, he said, "Whatever you want, you won't get it. I've called the cops. They're on their way right now. And I'm holding a gun here. So I'm giving you five seconds to get out of my house and never come back. Got me?"

Calling Dane's bluff, the man staggered forward on stick legs, still holding his head, forcing Dane to backpedal toward the kitchen, the vacuum thrust out in front of him like a pistol.

"I said get out!"

The man ignored the warning and kept advancing, walking with the forced gait of someone severely arthritic, moving into a small patch of moonlight that spilled through a gap in the curtains. The pale blue light swam up his frame until he was solidly illuminated.

Tall. Elderly. Decrepit. Bloody.

Hurt.

Gunshot, Dane realized. Dear God, the old man had been shot in the head, was gushing blood like a ruptured water main through the gnarled fingers he held there. As the blood pooled on the carpet, it hit the shadows and spread out like oil rising from the earth.

Similarly, the Dust Buster hit the floor, shattered, and bounced away.

Dane's back found the wall behind him and stopped him short, his mouth open in a scream that could not find its voice. He didn't know what scared him more, that the man was in his home, or that he was still alive somehow. He'd heard stories of people taking a bullet to the head and living, but this wound looked too severe for such a miracle.

From upstairs, Matti continued to whisper, "He's bleeding on the rug on the rug . . . "

The wounded man drew closer, leaving a trail of gore behind him, until finally he loomed over Dane. His eyes were cloudy and dry, his skin cracked and flaky and sallow, his teeth angled all wrong as if he'd shoved them into his own gums without regard to symmetry. A sad smile spread across his face, denoting a pathos Dane couldn't place.

And that was the curious bit. Judging by the slight smile and aged frame, there was nothing actually malicious about him, not that Dane could tell anyway. If anything, the man looked . . . content. Not content with the gunshot wound, but . . . somehow . . . content with his role as a victim. As if he'd accepted it with a *que sera* attitude. He looked the way Dane's grandpa looked when he would sit alone in a lawn chair at the family get-togethers while everyone else played horseshoes and went swimming. Content to be forgotten, and occasionally patronized, because inside he was truly just happy to be watching his legacy, just happy to be there as a part of it all.

The bleeding man before Dane registered such contentment behind the gore. The sad eyes, the friendly smile, the non-threatening physique.

Dane swallowed hard and asked, "Are you okay? You're bleeding. I . . . my wife . . . I need to call an ambulance."

With some care, the figure took his hand away from the hole in his head, blood rushing to freedom, and pointed at a photo on the ground to Dane's right. It was leaning against the wall, along with some others, waiting to be packed up. Without looking, Dane knew which one it was, having placed it there not long ago. It showed him and Matti standing in the living room—this very room where I stand cornered by a dying man, he realized—wearing matching San Diego Chargers sweatshirts. Matti's mother had taken it during last year's playoffs.

"Who . . . who shot you? Let me help you. My phone is—"

Dane headed to the table but the old man moved in front of him, blocking his path. A burst of adrenaline rushed through Dane, but again, the man did not come off as threatening, just insistent.

"My phone . . . "

Shaking his head but still smiling, the man pointed to another of the photos, this one resting on the ground near Dane's foot, where Matti had left it while packing. Dane looked at it, made out what it was even in the darkness.

"What? The photo? It's . . . it's Matti and me at Christmas. I don't understand and I don't have time—"

As emphatically as the hurt man could muster, he pointed to the photo again, blood running off his hand onto the carpet, urging Dane to take another look.

"Okay." Dane bent down and picked up the photo. Even in the dim moonlight, the picture was as he remembered it, a jovial snapshot of the two of them holding up pairs of socks, taken with the timer setting on the camera. As he stared at it, remembering the day fondly, a sallow-skinned finger dotted with blood tapped the glass frame.

Dane ignored it. "I need my phone."

Again, the finger tapped the glass, tapped it in the same spot repeatedly, leaving a coppery fingerprint. Looking at the bloodied man, Dane shook his head to show his confusion.

Still smiling contentedly, the man wiped the blood off the picture's glass covering and tapped it again.

The fingerprint appeared again in the same spot.

The man pushed the picture closer to Dane's face, as if to say, look harder.

"This is crazy." Confused and scared, Dane tore the back off the frame and pulled the photo out, careful not to rip it. It was a good memory and he wanted to keep it safe, especially in light of the memories he'd be losing a day from now as he handed the house keys over to the new owners. He remembered that Christmas morning well, the way the tree looked in the living room, the way both he and Matti felt that the house was really beginning to feel like home. He remembered pulling out the socks and remarking how much they both needed them, laughing that they were officially grownups now for thinking that way.

Where the bloody fingerprint had been on the glass, there was a lensflare in the photo.

The finger tapped it.

"That? The camera . . . it's old, it does that—"

The bloody finger rose to the first photo again, the one with Dane and Matti in football sweatshirts, and pressed against it.

Dane bent and picked up the photo. Again, he found the familiar lens flare that was common in many of their photos. He'd meant to buy a new camera, but had never found the time. He put the photo back. Another photo near it, taken in the kitchen on Thanksgiving, also had the lens flare.

But the one under it did not. It was taken at Disneyland with the same camera, and was flawless.

Intent to prove whatever point he was out to prove, the man pointed toward the foyer. A multi-picture frame still hung near the front door, Dane knew, containing similar photos; it hadn't been packed yet. It had been due to get boxed up when their need to feel each other had gotten the better of them, drawing them to the stairs where they made love.

"I have to help my wife, I can't—"

The old man shook his head no and pointed to the foyer again.

Hastily, Dane went to the frame in the foyer and

looked at it. Even in the darkness of the room, he could see the man reflected in the glass behind him, his face still a mass of red, pointing to one of the photos in the upper corner. It was taken in the kitchen as well, a picture of Dane drinking a Budweiser.

Lens flare.

Beneath it, a photo taken outside a nightclub.

No flare

Picture in the bedroom.

Lens flare.

From upstairs, Matti's voice filled the foyer, quick as ever and still hushed. "He's bleeding on the rug on the rug on the rug." Then, without breaking tempo, the refrain changed, causing Dane to spin and look up the stairs. "I shot him. I didn't mean to, the gun just went off. Please hurry, I love him. He's bleeding on the rug . . . "

The timbre was clearly Matti, but it sounded as if she were trying to mimic someone. She was good at mimicking people. She did it at parties sometimes. She could do Holly Golightly like it was nobody's business. But this was not a game. This was something else.

What spread through Dane next was not terror, or fear, or panic, or even more confusion, as he would have expected, but disbelief. The sum of all the parts was falling into place, painting a picture he found hard to digest. After all, he did not believe in ghosts

The gun-shot man, seeing Dane's wheels spinning, began to nod approvingly. He closed his eyes as his smile perked up at the sides, his blood now hitting the hardwood floor of the foyer. And with the sadness in his eyes suddenly making sense to Dane, he put a hand to Dane's shoulder and squeezed it reassuringly.

The touch was very faint, Dane noticed, like someone rubbing a feather on the spot. But it was frigidly cold, almost to the point of burning.

The old man followed this with a wave, a telltale wave that said, it's been a pleasure. And with that, turned and headed through the entryway into the living room.

The squeeze, the wave, the turn . . . it was an unmistakable universal gesture.

Saying goodbye, Dane realized. He's saying goodbye.

The lights flickered once and came on. Dane rushed into the living room, but the man was gone, just like that, taking the bloodstains with him. The carpet was as clean as it had been before he'd gone to bed.

Everything was silent.

Nothing was out of place. The boxes, the trash bags, the stacks of items waiting to be packed, all were exactly as they'd left them. He sat on a box of books he'd packed just a few hours earlier, full of Matti's horror novels, and looked around him for answers. Did all that really just happen? He felt light headed, a little dizzy. Was what he'd just seen real, or was he imagining things?

He touched the box, thinking of the contents inside, and what he'd just experienced. Horror. The supernatural. Ghosts. Such bullshit. Matti joked that she read them for insurance—Ed Lee and Jack Ketchum and a bunch of other names that meant nothing to him—read them so she'd know what to do if she ever found herself staring down a demon. She once re-marked she might be psychic. Said she was like a char-acter in one of those books. Nonsense, he'd replied, that crap is warping your brain. Psychics are just frauds looking for money. It ain't real.

Right?

"Dane? Where are you?"

Oh God, he realized, Matti's awake!

He took the stairs two at a time, this time knocking over a box of knick knacks, and rushed into the bed-room. Matti was sitting up, rubbing her eyes, feeling the empty spot in the bed next to her. She was all right, her complexion back to normal.

"What are you doing?" she asked. "It's almost four in the damn morning. I told you we'll finish packing tomorrow. The truck isn't coming till noon. Stop freak-ing out about it."

"Yeah, baby," he said, kissing her head and rubbing her hair, feeling how much she was a necessary part of his life. "It's just...um . . . you were talking in your sleep."

"Oh please, not that again. What'd I say this time?"

"Um . . . well . . . nothing. I'll tell you in the morning."

"Good. I'm exhausted." Matti rolled over and curled up in a fetal position, finding one of the small bears that kept residence around her pillow and pulling it toward her. "Come cuddle me," she said.

"Hey, baby?" Dane put his arm around her and

drew her into him, spooning.

Matti grunted.

"We never did get the history of this house before we moved in, did we?"

Another grunt.

"I love this house, you know. I always felt comfortable here for some reason. I mean, nothing ever went wrong here. Everything always worked, I always felt safe, I never really felt . . . alone here. You ever feel that?"

"Mmmm."

A minute passed, Dane lightly rubbing his hand down is wife's warm back, rethinking his attitude toward the unknown. As her breathing shifted to the even rhythm of sleep, he asked quietly, as much for himself as for Matti or anyone else listening, "You ever think there are people in this world who are just happy to be around other people? Content to watch silently as things go on around them? Just staying out of the way. You think they get sad when people leave them?"

Matti managed a final comment before she began to snore. "I dunno, Dane. I'm tired. Does it matter?"

He let her drift into her dreams before answering: "Kinda. I think I just met one."

Downstairs, the kitchen phone began to buzz as the line came back to life.

Looking at the clock, he thought, two hours until I have to get up.

SQUEAKY WHEELS

EVERYONE WHO LIVED on Hill Drive was standing outside the entrance to Cottonwood Park, chattering like squirrels. Police cruisers were parked at random, up on the curbs, blocking the street, attempting a semblance of barriers. Even in the daylight, their lights played on the nearby treetops. Dogs in the back yards of adjacent houses ran in circles and barked.

George huffed and maneuvered his unmarked sedan through the crowd of lookieloos, muttering curses under his breath. "Outta the way, idiot. Don't you see the frigging car about to run you over." Cruiser Jockeys were doing their best to control the small neighborhood crowd but were spread too thin to cover all the entrances to the park, i.e. the two miles of unfenced tree line that ran the perimeter. He parked near Ted Newcomb's car, took his gun and holster from the seat next to him and got out. A group of kids on bikes were discussing how to sneak into the woods from a back street. George stabbed a finger at them. "I find you in there near that scene I'm arresting you." He strapped his shoulder holster in place, punctuating the threat. They didn't look too frightened. Brats. "Go on, get out of here."

They pedaled off, no doubt still intent on their plan.

There was no clear path into the woods (these things never happened in the open areas near swings and slides) but a steady stream of officers coming and going through the trees pointed out the way to the crime scene. He walked into the woods, brushing away limbs as he went. Radios were hissing and popping, bouncing off tree trunks, growing louder as he pushed deeper. He stepped into a small dirt clearing, found Ted Newcomb instructing a uniformed officer to cordon off the area with yellow police tape.

"Hey, Ted."

"George. You hear the call?"

"When I was getting my donut like a good cop. So what do we got? I heard something about rats?"

"Oh, we got rats. Lots of 'em. Take a look over there in that big pit."

George stepped inside the perimeter of the police tape, heard the squeaking noises coming from the pit before he saw the source. The pit was easily ten by ten feet wide, and some eight or nine feet deep. Manmade. He didn't know what was more disturbing, that some-one had dug the equivalent of a grave in a neighbor-hood park, or the way the floor was moving. A writhing sea of rats filled the pit, hundreds of them, scurrying in a panic over one another, squealing and desperately try-ing to climb up the sides. The ones that weren't trying to escape were occupied with something else: a female corpse, half eaten, bloated and gray, slick with decom-position. George watched one of the frenzied rodents gnawed a chunk of skin off the top of the corpse's head and felt his stomach turn. He picked up a rock and hurled it at the rat but missed completely. Baseball was not his thing. No doubt Mandy would take up softball just to annoy him. He turned back to Ted. "Jesus. I won't be able to eat donuts for a week."

"Good, you could stand to lose the weight."

"I'm serious, this is fucking-A disgusting. Where's the M.E.?"

"That one over there," Ted pointed to a young officer who looked fresh from the academy, "said he was on the way. Animal control is on their way too."

"He get here first?" George indicated the same young cop.

"No, another unit. They're out on the street now."

"They talk to you?"

"Yeah. Said some kids—"

"Kids?"

"Yeah, kids, twelve and thirteen . . . that still count as kids these days?"

"Shit, I hope so. Mandy's only ten. I ain't ready for a grandkid just yet. Can those rats get out of there?"

"Well, they haven't yet. Not that they aren't giving it the old college try."

"Someone made this. Put the rats in there. You think?"

"It's a likely theory." Ted nodded, picked something out of his teeth. "Filled it with rats and dropped this woman in it. Let them eat her to death."

"Homicide. Trying to cover something up?"

"Hell of a lot of trouble to go to to get rid of a corpse."

George hated his next thought, but voiced it anyway. "Did it while she was alive? Torture?"

"The world is insane."

"The world *is* insane. Wait, what about the kids?"

Ted was done picking his teeth, wiped his hands on his blazer. "Kids were out here lighting off fire-crackers. Found this pit covered with some tree trunks. Those right there." A series of felled logs ringed the makeshift grave. Orange cones were ringed around them, denoting they were somehow evidence. "Heard some squeaking noises coming from under them. Fig-ured it was an animal and slid it over to look. Saw the rats. Saw the—"

"Saw the corpse and ran. Okay, I can figure it out. Where are they now, the kids?"

"Sitting in on one of the squad cars waiting for their parents to come down so they can make a statement."

"Great. I love when parents get involved. Just end up confusing their own kids."

"I dunno, my brother's kid eats cat food. Wouldn't want him as a character witness at my trial. Picks his nose all the time too—"

"Did they see anyone else hanging around? People not from the neighborhood?"

"Not that I know of. Perp could have come from anywhere. The park technically stops about a mile that way, but the woods continue down to the river where the lye factory is. So the guy could have parked at the factory and hoofed it through the woods all the way up here. We're checking the employee list but I'm not hold-ing out for a hero."

"They say anything off the record?"

Ted shook his head no. "Just what I told you. The trees, the squeaks, the leftovers as you see them."

"They recognize her?"

"Can anybody recognize that?"

"Okay, I'll go talk to them. I can't look at this thing anymore."

Ted threw up a palm. "Hang on."

"What?"

"Check this out first." Ted motioned to a patch of dirt at the edge of the clearing. A set of tracks wound out of the foliage and lead to the pit. "Kids said they didn't do it."

George had seen this type of track before. Most homicide detectives had at one point in their career. "Looks like a drag pattern. Couple of footprints here. Guy must have whacked her somewhere else, dragged the body out here."

"Knocked her out anyway. There's no bullet hole on her I can see. And I'm not getting down in that pit to look further."

"So we know he came from that direction," George said, pointing into the belly of the woods. "That near the lye factory?"

"Near the river anyway. But that's not what I'm looking at. See there's this drag mark here, and then there's this skinnier one that runs between the foot prints. Could be another—"

"Some fucking prints. What're those marks there?"

"I'm thinking telephone pole guy. 's'why I don't think he's a factory worker. You know the guys got those spikes on their boots?"

"Yeah. Climb the poles with 'em. Gotcha. So a cable or telephone guy. Maybe parked at the factory after closing. Kept the boot climbers on for traction. Let's check and see if any service was done in the area recently."

"I already put the word out on that, too. But this thin drag line here, this is what concerns me. See how it skids about? Separate from the other drag mark."

"Like something was moving," George replied, suddenly more stressed, "maybe trying to get free. You think it's another body?"

"I certainly hope not. If we're looking for a second victim . . ."

George stood up and looked around the woods. They seemed to stretch on forever. "And if this guy has more of these pits . . ."

The young cop leaned over the police tape and yelled, "Hey, detectives? Animal Control is here!"

● ● ●

Sleep was not something Ted Newcomb got during these kinds of cases. It was one thing to find a DOA with a gunshot or stab wound, but torture victims burned afterimages in his mind that took years to scrub away. And so he stirred all night and tried to rationalize it all. Which was a futile exercise in the end. The world was sick, and there was no solution. Even if he did catch this guy, legal council would just convince the jury he was abused as a kid and deserved to spend his days in a padded room with a soft cot and three square meals. It was bullshit.

The M.E.'s report was on his desk the next morning. No other leads had come in since the body's discovery yesterday afternoon. The employee list for the factory had been secured and officers had questioned everyone on it throughout the night. Turned out they were all married, and all had alibis. All of them. They were told not to leave town anyway. But Ted knew, people lie. He would follow up on them all tomorrow.

He filed it in his briefcase, started going through his other notes. There were so many that he still needed to weed through. He'd gotten home late and had talked to so many people yesterday his head was still dizzy. Maybe the telephone/cable worker angle would pan out. He made another call to the cable companies, asked for a list of employees. The cable company said it was contacting their lawyer and would get back to him asap. Swore their employees were screened and bonded.

It was ten before George showed up, a cup of coffee in his hands. He didn't look like he'd slept any better. Said something about needing to spend the morning with his little girl after yesterday's find. Wasn't the best work acumen to have, but Ted understood. You see enough dead bodies you begin to wonder when you're number's coming up. George was eligible for early retirement and had been talking about moving his family someplace warmer, buying a boat, finding Mandy a good school and a safe place to grow up. If such a place existed anymore.

Ted maneuvered through the desks and plopped down in a chair next to George. He took out his notes and started leafing through them. "I got the report from the M.E. Our Jane Doe is Shelly Dumas, lived two streets over from the park. Single, no kids, traveled a lot for work so no one in the neighborhood would really know if she was missing or not. She did real estate, worked for herself. So no boss or friends calling to find out why she wasn't in work. Blunt force trauma to the head. But the rats definitely killed her. At least, that's the definitive cause of death. No way to look for hemorrhaging. Chewed her up, sent her into shock, she bled out and died. Ate half her flesh and most of her internal organs. Has more germs in her now than they have text books for. CDC is flying someone in to take a closer look, just to be safe. M.E. puts her decomp at about two days."

George sipped coffee from his I LOVE DADDY mug. "Jesus. And forensics?"

"Place was clean of trace save for about a gazillion rat hairs. They took a mold of the prints, seconded the idea the guy has boots with spikes on them. Someone speculated the skinnier drag marks could be a small body, maybe a kid, judging by the way it slides. 'Could be' is the thing. Could also be a suitcase or his laundry for all we know. Neighborhood kids are all accounted for anyway."

"Well thank God for that."

"No forced entry at Dumas' home. Lots of prints on her property, but she's single so who knows how many guys she's had over. We're running them all through the system. So far nothing. Guy who fills a pit with rats, though? No way he left his prints."

"No shit."

Ted flipped through more of his notes. "Otherwise, nothing out of place, no signs of struggle."

"Guy cased her house, waited for her to come out?"

"Neighbors have seen her jogging in the past. Makes sense. She goes out for a jog, the guy grabs her, hits her over the head, drags her into the trees—"

"Feeds her to the rats. The sick fuck. Rape?" George asked.

"Nope."

"Anything on the telephone pole lead?"

"Nope."

"Missing persons reports from surrounding areas?"

"Nope."

"They find anything else in the woods? Another pit?"

"Nope."

"Say nope again."

"Nope."

• • •

A press conference was scheduled for two o'clock in one of the meeting rooms at the station. A select group of media was invited to come hear what information was being released to the public. Mostly this would consist of a profile and a warning for people in the neighborhood.

The rat angle had already made it out; the kids had seen to that.

Ted was meeting with someone from animal control to get specifics about the rats, so George headed to the conference where the chief was already answering questions for the news cameras. He stood to the side and listened, played with his tie out of anxious habit.

"What about police presence?" A young blonde female reporter from one of the local stations.

"We have units patrolling twenty-four-seven," the chief responded. "But people are asked to not go near the woods alone, and to report any suspicious activity they see. We can't be everywhere at once."

"Why not go near the woods?" Another reporter, a young guy prematurely balding. "The killer still lurking around?"

"Not likely, but you know about the rats. We don't know if any got out. We don't need a rabies epidemic on our hands."

"What efforts are underway to find out who this guy is?" A newspaper reporter with a tape recorder raised up. She's cute, George thought. Maybe I should have waited to get married.

"We've got some leads. We're checking them out.

We'll let you know what we find."

"And what if the guy left town? How do you find him then? And what if he's planning on coming back? Can't you tell us anything?"

"We're looking. Trust us."

"You can't just tell the people you'll find him when you've got nothing tangible to show them right now."

Cuteness aside, George didn't like this girl's attitude, the way she was out to make the chief stumble so people would grumble about the ineptitude of the force. It was always the same song and dance. The media wanted to look like they were more concerned than the men who put their lives on the line every day, even though what they really wanted was a juicy story to lure advertisers with. "Look," George said from the side of the room. Everyone turned to him. The chief was clearly annoyed at the interruption, but George and he went way back; he'd get over it. "Look," he continued. "You want some kind of pledge? I'm telling you. I'm gonna find this guy if he goes to the moon. So quit displacing anger. We're gonna get him. And if I find him first . . . God help him." Just for good measure, he turned to the television cameras. "Yeah, if you're watching, I'm gonna get you."

He walked out of the room. Someone behind him made a statement about cops watching too many movies. The Chief apologized and tried to field more questions.

There'd be hell to pay for that little stunt, but George didn't care. All he wanted was a goddamn boat anyway.

● ● ●

"Hi, detective." Julia Green, Director of Animal Management, met Ted at her office downtown. She was much more attractive than her phone voice led on, especially for someone who specialized in rodent control. Long red hair, fair skin, small nose, and a body that came from time spent in a gym. Ted's eyes fell to her hands and scanned for rings, but they were bare. Maybe he'd call her later, ask her for a drink. He was getting jealous of George's stories about happy matrimony. He wanted someone to watch TV with, someone to grill hamburgers for. Even someone to bicker with. *Admit it, Ted, you're lonely.* He took a seat near her desk, read the diplomas on the wall as she sat down and fired up her computer.

"So, detective—"

"Call me Ted."

"Okay, Ted, your office faxed over a copy of the medical examiner's report about this Dumas woman. Grotesque. And terribly disturbing. You have no idea who did it?"

"We're hoping you can help us. What can you tell me about the rats?"

"They're quarantined right now until CDC can get to them."

"That's fine. I saw enough of them yesterday."

"The species in question is *rattus norvegicus*."

"Norviwhat?"

"Brown rats. Wild rats. An aggressive breed

amongst themselves, but relatively harmless when domesticated."

"Were these domesticated?"

"No, they weren't. They're way too aggressive."

Ted smiled. He hoped he looked charming. "Of course."

"It gets weirder."

"We passed weird a long time ago. We're in Bizarro World now."

"What?"

"Nothing. A Superman joke. What's weirder than what we've already got?"

"Well, it was a lot of rats, both bucks and does . . . and they weren't angry at one another."

Ted waited for the weird part, and when she didn't say anything more, figured that must have been it. "Okay, should they be?"

"Rats don't like other rats that much. That's where most of their aggression goes. They live in small groups, families. It's possible a family of rats could grow this large, but I've never heard of it."

"Really? Ever seen *Willard?*"

"Of course. They call me the 'rat girl' 'round here. I see all the rat films, mostly so I can sit and argue how inaccurate they are."

"I'm the same with cop films. You know how many times I've fired my gun? None. Not once. Just at the shooting range. But Mel Gibson—"

"So you see my point. In movies they use farm-raised domesticated species. But this . . . this was a lot of wild rats."

"But don't all rats live in the wild together?"

"Rats are territorial, usually led by a dominant male, and they'll section off areas of the woods. When a rat from one group meets a rat from another group they will fight. Almost always to the death or until one gives up and runs away. All these rats together . . . not fighting . . . "

"So then this *was* all the same family?"

"Has to be." Julia Green suddenly looked very concerned.

"But feels like too many rats for one family to you."

She nodded. "To me, yes."

"Hence, the weird part."

"Bizarro, as you put it. Different families in a hole together . . . it's possible a new dominant male is established and they work it out. Not very likely, but possible. I wouldn't put money on it."

"So our guy definitely knows rats, because he wouldn't want them to kill each other. It would defeat his purpose. He needed them alive to eat . . . " He stopped before his words drew a picture of the half-eaten woman. "You think he figured out a way to get different rat families to get along?"

"People have weird hobbies, detec—Ted. One thing's for sure, whoever handled them is a courageous man. A bite from a wild brown rat can cause all sorts of problems: Salmonella, trichinosis, hanta virus, Weils Disease, the list goes on."

"But people have rats as pets, yes?"

"Sure. But again, those are domesticated, raised in stores. They're vaccinated. These weren't."

"Brown rats. They normal for these parts?"

"To all of America just about. Want a statistic? There's always a rat within fifteen meters of a human."

"I don't do meters, sorry."

"About fifty feet."

Ted suddenly noticed everything that was fifty feet from him. Were they in the heating vents even now? "Too close for comfort."

"So, yes, there are rats in the park," Julia continued. "But for all of them to end up in a man-made pit like that . . . "

"What if the guy caught them, kept them at his house or something till he was ready to use them?"

"Still a stretch. That many rats . . . there are no homes in these parts secluded enough someone wouldn't see, hear or smell something. Rats mark their territory. It's pretty foul. The stench alone would garner attention. Honestly, I'm at a loss as to how he got them to co-exist. There are missing pieces of a puzzle here I don't think I can fill in for you. Sorry."

Ted smiled again, going for more charm. "Just out of curiosity, about how long would it take these brown rats to kill someone?"

"I don't really know. You have to understand it's rare for a rat to bite a human. Generally only when people are sleeping and if the rat is very hungry or defending itself. But in this case, if the girl was unconscious, once the biting started . . . they have powerful incisors. They cut through meat quickly."

"But how long?"

"I can't say for sure how long. I don't even know of any cases where people have been killed by rats. It's usually the diseases, or the mites and fleas that cause the most damage. And almost all of it is curable with antibiotics. But, if I'm speculating, it would be slower than you would hope. Hours. Days. At least until the body shuts down from shock. It would take a long time."

She paused, reflecting on what she was saying. Ted could see her forming a mental image in her head. Welcome to my world, he thought.

"Dear God," she finally said, "I hope you catch this guy."

"We're trying."

Minutes later he left, without her number.

●   ●   ●

For the rest of the day, every news station in the city replayed George's arrogant challenge to the killer. The chief was livid. Ted could hear him screaming at George even now in his office, ordering him out to fix this "fuckjob of a mess."

Ted, who was on the phone talking to the telephone company, had to put a finger in his free ear to hear the guy on the other end. But the conversation was soon exhausted so he said bye and hung up.

George exited the chief's office, stopped at Ted's

desk. "What'd the phone company say?"

"What do you think? There was no service scheduled in the area, but they're gonna get us a list of employees anyway. I'm calling the cable companies next. They're being hard asses."

George hooked a thumb over his shoulder back toward the chief's office. "You hear that? I think we're breaking up."

"He'll get over it. Buy him some roses."

"You think I should have been quiet at the briefing?"

"I only know what they're showing on TV, George. Which is you directly challenging this guy. You might want to think of Mandy and your wife here."

"I am, that's why I did it. How do they have faith in me otherwise?"

"Faith shmaith. How about they live in peace rather than look over their shoulders for the rest of their lives because you pissed off some psycho pied piper."

"You don't understand."

Ted leaned back in his chair. "Enlighten me."

George stood mute, playing with his tie. "Aw, fuck it. I'm going to check on those kids again, see if I can get their parents to shut up this time. Let me know what you find out."

• • •

It was nearly nine o'clock when George left the Burke home, apologizing once more for interrupting their dinner, though he really couldn't care that he had. Ralph Burke was one of the boys who'd moved the logs to find the body. George had finally gotten the kid to open up without the parent's interrupting, and that was good. It made him eager to get home and see Mandy, maybe play a board game with her.

The radio station was playing his sound bite again as he pulled onto the main road. His wife was going to give him hell for it as well. Hopefully Mandy hadn't heard it; she was only beginning to suspect what his job was really like. He turned it off and called Ted on his cell, eager to relay the Burke kid's new story.

Ted answered on the second ring. "George, what's up?"

"Listen to this. I went back to interview the kids . . . Hang on, I'm driving. Move it, pal! Don't flip me off I'll fucking shoot you!"

"George—"

"These idiots and their wannabe race cars."

"—what about the kids?"

"Okay, so the Burke kid, Ralph, him and his buddy Jason hang out in the woods a lot. They got a fort made out of some pallets they lean against a tree. Ralph says the other night he's skateboarding near the woods as the sun's going down and remembers he left something in the fort."

"So he goes in to get it."

"Right. Hang on, I'm gonna fucking kill this guy."

"Just change lanes."

"Okay, so he goes in to get his toy, some damn Star

Wars thing or something, and anyway, when he's in the fort, he hears someone coming."

"He's in the fort now?"

"Yeah. He peeks out through the slats in the pallet and sees a guy in a trench coat."

"A trench coat? I love it. Do these guys buy a pervert starter kit or something?"

"A big guy, moving through the woods, about to pass by the fort. The guy's breathing hard, like he's sick or something, and he's kind of hunched over and he's dragging something but the kid can't see what it is. He stops outside the fort for a sec, right near the slats."

"What's the kid do?"

"Just freezes. It's dark, he's already scared to be in the woods at sundown, and he's supposed to be home for dinner. His mother piped in at this point and confirmed he wasn't home. Says he closed his eyes and a few seconds later he opens them and looks out again and sees the guy moving off in the direction of the street. And get this, the moonlight catches him for a second . . . the guy's wearing some kind of Halloween mask."

"Jesus. What a freak. Why didn't the kid tell us this yesterday?"

"Says his dad told him to be quiet. I told you parents are fucking retarded. They need to pass a law about parental interference. I just knew he was holding something back."

"You're a parent."

"Hardy har."

"He seen the guy before?" Ted asked.

"First time."

"So now what, we put an APB out on a guy in a monster mask. He can't be stupid enough to wear it in public."

"You never know," George replied.

"I'm gonna call for a unit and head back to the park. Sounds like this guy knows his way around the woods. Maybe there are paths we missed, some clues the trace team overlooked."

"I'm way ahead of you," George said, steering his car down Hill Drive.

"What do you mean? Where are you?"

"Just got to the park."

"Already? Who's on patrol?"

"I dunno. I called in but there's no one here yet.'

●　●　●

Halfway across town in the drive-thru of a Wendy's, Ted went silent, the cell phone hot against his ear. What did George mean by 'yet?' Then it hit him. He checked his watch, saw that it was shift-changing time. There'd be a good ten to twenty minutes where the streets would be empty of squad cars. "George, don't be stupid. Wait for me."

"Look, we still don't know what that other drag mark is. If he's got someone else in there I'm not waiting. Besides, this theatrical shit . . . how well can a man see in a rubber mask? I'll surprise him." The line went dead.

"George? George? Shit." Ted threw his cell phone down on the car seat next to him, drove out of the drive-thru, nearly clipping the car in front of him.

• • •

I should be wearing sneakers, George thought, as he pushed through the trees and brambles, heading back to the pit in the woods. The flashlight he carried threw a bright white circle on everything, changing black shadows to brown and green plant life, but did nothing to ease maneuverability through the twisting foliage. In his other hand he carried his Glock, the safety off just in case; if this masked psycho was out here, he wasn't about to be taken by surprise.

God, he just wanted a boat and to be done with all this shit. Part of him knew it was stupid to be out here like Rambo, and he could hear Ted's lecture already, but the other part of him knew that if he ever planned to watch Mandy grow up normal, he had to be sure the world was a little safer. This rat guy was every guy that hurt women, and he wanted his daughter to know that her daddy was a safe haven when she needed it.

You're losing it, George.

He kept moving. Why didn't the police clear this path better yesterday? How the hell did they get the corpse and all those rats out of here without tripping over all these damn roots and thorn bushes? Did he even own sneakers?

Zzzzz. "Gah." He swatted a large mosquito out of his ear. He regretted making the noise, but he couldn't do anything about it now. Damn bugs. He hated bugs. Mandy loved them, caught them and put them in jars. She was a bit of a tomboy, but that was okay, it meant they could do guy things together. He made a mental note to take her fishing sometime soon.

Snick.

He stopped. That wasn't a bug, that was a twig snapping. Off to the left somewhere. His muscles went tight as ropes. His heart pumped.

Someone else walking in the woods?

Raising the gun, he waited silently, clicked off the flashlight and let his ears be his surveillance tool. The *skree* of insects filled the darkness. Tree limbs scratching one another in the light breeze. The susurration of leaves chafing above him. Nothing much else to note. Maybe it was a raccoon or something. Lots of four-legged things in these woods. After another minute of relative silence he breathed out and let the gun fall near his side again. "Okay," he whispered, a self-mocking code: *don't be such a pussy.*

The pit was about fifty yards to his north. He made it there without incident, his shoes now covered in dirt and moss. The police tape still surrounded the pit. A sign had been posted explaining the heap of shit anyone would be in if they felt like tampering with the scene.

"Ridiculous. Shoulda put men outside."

The department had ruled against leaving officers in the woods, said it was just impractical. They'd need lights and a shelter and a hundred other things on hand they didn't have. Their solution, in the absence of patrolling black and whites inside the trees, was to post similar signs like this one around the park, and drop notices in mailboxes. Which, George knew, was like sending everyone invitations to come out and fuck it all up.

George ducked under the police tape and shined his light into the pit. The hordes of rats were gone. Only dark red dirt, a couple of ladders leaning against the sides for authorities to get in and out. Other than that it looked like a large hole dug for coffins.

Snick!

There it was again. Another twig snapping. Close by. Was the guy actually in the woods again? Was he following George? These kind of serial nutballs, they tended to listen to the news. He'd been banking on that when he'd made his statement. Let the guy come to him, and they could work it out between themselves . . . with some bullets.

He threw caution to the wind. "Listen, you fuck, you want me you better come get me. 'Cause if I get you first . . . "

George raised his gun and moved off in the direction of the sound. *Snick.* There it was again, straight ahead. And was that breathing he heard? Or just the leaves rustling in the wind?

He made it a few more feet before the bushes to his left exploded in a torrent of flying twigs and leaves and a lumbering figure screamed out of the greenery and tackled him like a runaway freight train, slamming him to the ground with a thud that rattled his teeth. His breath was forced from his lungs. He fought to suck in air, to scream, but he couldn't. A trench coat flapped before his eyes, reflecting the flashlight's beam before it fell to the ground and shut off. Then the man was wailing on him, beating him in the ribs, breaking them with each blow. *Crack crack crack!* George felt himself crying. Something long, hard and gray—a fucking fire hose?—

    caught him in the testicles and rolled him up into a fetal position. Pain running up his abdomen. The man on him again, pounding, pounding, slamming George's head into the dirt, huffing and grunting like he had wet socks jammed down his throat. The smell of something vitriol—urine?—saturating the air. George's radio was in his jacket, turned down so the static wouldn't give him way. He needed to get it out. He reached—

The man grabbed his arm, twisted it and snapped the bones at the elbow.

"AHH!" His were eyes out of his head.

Fight back, George, fight back. You're gonna die! Get the radio. Get it.

In the midst of the tumbling, his punches failing to connect, his feet scrambling for footing, he caught a glimpse of the assailant's Halloween mask in the moonlight.

And he thought, "Ra—"

• • •

Ted pulled up next to George's car at the south entrance to the park. The local news radio station was replaying the day's earlier conference. Goddamn George was everywhere.

Way to make yourself a target, George.

He hopped out and shined his light inside George's car. The computer was on, a cup of coffee in the drink holder. The handheld radio was gone. Everything else looked normal. "Stupid, George. Real fucking asinine."

He went back to his own car, called in and requested a cruiser jockey come by regardless of what the shift change status was. "Give 'em overtime," he instructed, "but get a car out here now."

Then he headed into the woods.

Mosquitoes attacked him as soon as he got beyond the tree line. What the hell was George trying to prove going into the woods alone? Why did he even think this freak would be hanging around in them late at night right after the cops had swarmed the place? The guy was probably long gone if he knew what was good for him. Would probably lay low for a year or two and then pop up again in a nearby town. Maybe here, if he was the sort of crazy who needed the attention. And judging by the rat-pit MO, yeah, he was that sort of crazy.

"Gonna kill you when I find you, George," Ted said, shoving aside a low limb.

The thick undergrowth of the woods was worse to get through than the damn obstacle course he'd been forced to run back at the academy some ten lifetimes ago. Jump this boulder, duck this branch, kick through these brambles. Jeez, he was already exhausted.

Shuffling noises nearby spoke of animals racing to get away from him as he moved. Every fifty feet, he remembered. Good thing he hadn't asked what the diseases did to a person, curable or not. He shuddered at the thought he might even step on one of the damn things. Seeing all those rats in one pit was creepy enough. To imagine there were any around him now just plain gave him the heebeie jeebies.

His flashlight's battery was dying, the beam a yellow coffee ring on the trees. Great, like I'll be able to see any rats now if it dies, he thought.

The pit had to be getting closer, he hoped, maybe another hundred yards. Nothing looked familiar in the darkness of the woods. Just a lot of frigging branches. The cops should have cleared a goddamn path. This was just about futile at this time of night. This was—

He stopped dead in his tracks when he heard the groaning.

"Hello?"

The groaning grew louder. Someone in pain. Ted undid the snap on his shoulder holster, took his gun out. Cautiously, he followed the groaning, which drew him in the direction of the pit.

"Oooooh."

"George? That you?" It sure as hell sounded like George. But there was a new sound now, a hitch-pitched squealing. Like a car with bad brakes. It was getting louder, closer.

Adrenaline coursed through Ted's veins as he raced through the woods, ignoring the limbs whipping him in the face. The pit swam into view, moonlight rippling down through the tree canopy into the clearing, illuminating the police tape.

"Ooo . . ."

"George!" Ted ripped the tape with his hand, stepped past it and looked into the pit.

George was lying at the bottom, his legs and arms bent at 90-degree angles, but not the way God intended them to. "Jesus Christ, George. What happened?"

George was wide-eyed; his face was a mass of contusions.

Now the high-pitched squeal stopped. Something rushed through the woods behind Ted, swishing the leaves, drumming the ground, then was gone.

Ted spun around, his flashlight bouncing faint shadows over the surrounding trees. Everything was so damn dark. Where the hell was the guy? He'd shoot him on sight.

He spoke over his shoulder, keeping an eye on the woods. "George, just hang on, there's a car on its way. Give it a minute. Is this our guy? Do you know which way he went?"

A grunt. Sounded like *I don't know.*

Got to be here somewhere, Ted thought. Just heard him a second ago. He's not as stealthy as he thinks.

The running footsteps came out of nowhere to his right. He turned to shoot. Something slammed into him. A trench coat. A rat mask. White erupted under his eyes. The floor of the pit came up and rammed into his body.

His back shrieked in pain and he went stiff, barely able to move, the wind knocked out of him.

Get up get up get up, he told himself. His gun, torn from his grip when he'd landed, was a dark spot on the dirt. The flashlight was nowhere in sight, probably still up above the pit. Reaching out, he snatched up the gun. He rolled over, ignored the pain that flared up his spine, and aimed up.

Nothing. Just treetops and the silver dollar moon beyond.

On the ground to his right, George was grunting hysterically. He seemed . . . genuinely scared.

Where was the guy? Ted swung the gun all around the edge of the pit, waiting for a shadow to appear. There was no getting up, he knew that, his back was sprained or broken or something. The guy had hit him with such force it nearly knocked his brains lose.

Then there was sound. Something moving around up at the edge of the pit, something dragging its feet through the dirt.

Show yourself, thought Ted, gun aimed.

As if in response, something long and gray flipped over the edge, wound itself around the nearest ladder and yanked it out in the blink of an eye. More shuffling, and the gray hose-like thing found the other ladder and yanked it out as well. Then, whatever the hose-like thing was appeared over the edge once more, just dangling, yet moving ever so slightly on its own. What the hell is that, thought Ted? A snake? Now it swished back and forth, twitching, the movement unmistakable. Both he and George stared at it disbelieving.

A tail. One hell of a large fucking tail. Boy, this guy went all out on the costume.

"Come on, you shithead," Ted yelled. "Stick your head over the edge. I just want to see your stupid mask." He held the gun out, still aiming, just looking for one good opportunity to fire.

The tail disappeared.

Silence.

Then, more shuffling.

Next to him, George became frantic. Grunting, almost screaming.

Ted looked at him, barely visible in the moonlight, followed his friend's gaze up toward the edge of the pit on the north side. Something black was sliding out over the edge. Oblong, moving cautiously, titling downward.

Slowly, a rat's head swam into view, looking down on them. A giant rat's head. Bigger than a human head. More like the size of a horse's head. Damn, that looks real, Ted thought.

He fired, but the shot went wide and missed. The recoil screamed through his back and he damn near fainted from the pain.

The rat's head opened its mouth. Wide. Wider. Its incisors like yellow swords.

Ted was confused. How the hell did the guy get the

mouth to open like that? How'd he get the tongue and teeth to move? How—

EEEEEEEEEEE!

The rat head shrieked, the nose twitching rapidly, the whiskers dancing, the eyes blinking.

George was crying.

And Ted's mind went a bit numb, because he was putting it all together now.

Not fake, he realized. Real. Oh God. Real. Dear God. How?

The drag marks and claw prints, the squealing noises: a giant rat with giant rat feet, dragging its tail behind. The pieces fell in place. But why the trench coat?

He heard his nephew's bratty voice: Because, stupid, when you're a giant rat in suburbia, survival is all about camouflage. How do you think it's lasted this long? Duh!

The treetops turned blue and red. The rat head looked up, hissed at the lights.

The police cruiser must be here, thought Ted. Oh Christ, hurry.

The giant rat looked back down at them, opened its mouth wide. Wider. As wide as it could go. And from its mouth, like projectile vomit, spilled forth a rush of brown rats, tumbling over one another as they fell. They poured into the pit and rose like water. Their sharp little nails zoomed over the two detectives lying prone on the ground. Ted Screamed. George screamed. The rats kept coming. One big family spawned from something unexplainable and evil.

Ted's scream became a shriek of sheer terror. The bites came quick. Too quick, according to what Julia Green had said. Uncharacteristically fast. His body lost control and flailed uselessly as it tried to deal with the pain. Where were the damn Cruiser Jockeys? Couldn't they hear the screams? Didn't they see his car? Or had they parked somewhere else?

Crunching sounds shot up from George's body. He cried incoherently, something that sounded like *Mandy*. Then his grunting and moaning stopped and only the crunching noises came.

The rats kept biting Ted. Tiny piercing stabs, shredding his flesh. Quick. But not quickly enough. How he envied George's silence.

Through the blood-thirsty frenzy of putrid pelts on his face, he saw the giant rat above tear off into the woods . . . right before a pair of one inch yellow incisors sank into his eyeballs.

He felt hot fluid run down his cheek as his vision darkened. He was mad at how wrong they'd been this time. He had so many questions. But the pain was everything now.

It took a long time to die.

COOKIES HAVE NO SOULS

THE THING ABOUT turning regular old chocolate chip cookies into living, breathing chocolate chip cookies, thought Raul as he pulled a screaming one from the jar, was that they seemed to go bitter while in captivity. Some of them were even able to pop their chocolate chips out, which some-how accelerated their decay. Raul was constantly picking loose chips out of the bottom of the cookie jar and throwing them out. Because what good was a chocolate chip cookie without any chips, living or not? Reaching into the jar was nerve-wracking, though, because the living chocolate chip cookies had teeth. Not sharp teeth, necessarily, but sharp enough to pinch the skin. A few times since he'd created them, some brave cookies had latched onto his thumb with their tiny fangs. Once, a large one got him, and when Raul yanked his hand out quickly, the cookie flew across the room and ran off. He never found it. And now, sometimes at night, he thought he heard it running in the walls.

The notion that tiny little chocolate chip cookie eyes were watching him as he slept gave him the willies. He'd find it someday, though. It couldn't outwit him forever.

"I want a big one," Tera said, reaching up toward her daddy as he pulled the cookie from the jar.

"Okay, pumpkin," Raul said, looking down at his four-year-old daughter. It was only recently that Raul deemed her old enough to eat the living cookies, showing her how to break them in half slowly until the faint screaming stopped. Only when the screaming ended was she allowed to lick the chocolate blood off her fingers, scoop out the teeth, and take a big bite.

"Bigger, Daddy," she said, "bigger."

Raul dropped the cookie he was holding back in the jar and reached for a larger one. The cookies scooted around as a pack and cowered against the curve of the jar, but could find no means of avoiding his large hand other than hiding underneath one another. The ones on top nipped at his fingers.

"Ah, I've got a really big one," he said, pulling out a cookie so large it had four blinking eyes. It wriggled frantically in his grip. "Look honey, a Siamese chocolate chip cookie." He chuckled.

"Gimme gimme," Tera shouted, jumping up and down. "I wanna eat it up. Gimme."

Raul handed her the cookie and told her to be careful of the second mouth. He watched in delight as his daughter slid her tongue between her lips—her concentration face—and stared the cookie down.

"I'm gonna eat you up," she said.

The cookie made a frantic attempt to wiggle away, its eyes wide with terror, but it could not break free. Slowly, methodically, Tera broke the cookie in half and let the chocolate blood ooze down her fingers.

Raul's own mouth watered as the cookie's four tiny eyes glossed over, as its faint "Eeeeee!" screaming faded to nothing. Freshly killed ones were so warm and soft--simply delectable.

Tera put the cookie in her mouth and bit into it, coating her teeth in chocolate goodness. As always, the other cookies jumped around the cookie jar like Mexican jumping beans, their teeth clicking in fear. Raul suspected they had some kind of psychic connection with one another, as if they could feel each other's pain. But then, cookies didn't really feel, did they?

When Tera was done, she ran to her bedroom, got her teddy bear, and jumped on the couch to watch TV, satisfied by her pre-dinner snack. Raul wanted a cookie too but could only have one per day--doctor's orders; he'd have to wait until after dinner for his.

He put the lid back on the jar and joined his daughter on the couch. Inside the jar, the cookies shivered in fear.

THE RUNNER AND
THE BEAST

PAUL COULDN'T EAT; he was too nervous. The potatoes and chicken on his plate were growing colder by the minute, and even though his stomach rumbled, he could not bring himself to touch the food. Instead, he looked out the window to the street, saw two men passing by in a horse-drawn cab. They held hands over their mouths, whispering cautiously, little clouds of warm breath pluming in the cold air.

Rising from the table, he moved to the fireplace and stoked the small flames. Night was falling and the temperature would only continue to drop. When would the land warm up, he wondered. It was almost spring and yet the maple trees and juniper bushes were still brown and bare. He could not remember a winter so grim. His neighbor had died from pneumonia just last week, a sweet old woman who'd called him Sir; she'd shivered like a flag whipping in a tempest breeze as he sat by her bed and prayed for her soul's wellbeing. The image burned in his mind as he rubbed his hands in front of the flames.

Tensions were high tonight. While out walking earlier he had seen people bolting their doors. Through their windows, they could be seen armed with stolen rifles and muskets. Their whispers were uniform: the British boats had left the docks, the roadblocks were increasing, the troops were amassing. England was unhappy with the colonies.

Again, he thought of the December snow and how cold it had been against his head in New Hampshire three months ago. The trek through the dense woods to the resistance had been arduous and exhausting, but it had been necessary to raid the garrison for ammunition. The law couldn't prove it was him, but they had their suspicions, and he knew it. He was being watched.

Satisfied with the fire's heat, he picked his hide coat up off the bed. It was good against the wind, if not a tad restricting, and when he donned it he felt the weight of the night rest on his shoulders. His tricorn hat lay next to it; he placed it on his head. Next, he slipped on a pair of cracked leather gloves, stained with the soil of numerous New England towns. He lit a candle on the dresser near his bed, watched the flame grow and lick. Such a small flame, he thought, and yet were it to fall to the floor, the house would burn to cinders. Could he be like that flame tonight, he asked himself.

Bang bang! He jumped. Someone was knocking at the door. The rifle on the table was in his hand in a flash. "Who is it?"

"Sir, it's me, Richard." The voice belonged to a young boy.

Richard, Paul thought, Dr. Warren's stable boy from the next town. When he opened the door, the boy spilled into the room with pluming breath, his cheeks flushed with blood. "Sir," he said, "they're on the move."

"Are you sure? You must be sure."

"Yes, sir. A whole army, coming this way. Close behind. More than we thought."

Paul grabbed the boy's shoulders and dragged him to the table. "Here, sit, eat."

"But I have to get back—"

"You'll go back when you're rested and full. Warm yourself by the fire."

"Won't they come here?"

"No, they're watching me. They'll see me leave."

Paul buttoned up his collar, gave the boy a squeeze on the shoulder. "You did well."

He turned to leave, his hand on the door handle, when the boy spoke again. "Sir?"

"Yes, Richard."

"Sir, stay out of the woods by the stream. I cut through and was followed. I heard footsteps following me the whole time. They may have set a trap."

"Good job, boy. Now eat."

Paul left.

● ● ●

Paul's instincts had been correct, as they often were; something was happening tonight. He briskly walked away from his home, staying in the center of the street, knowing he was being watched, hoping to draw any officials away from his house, away from the boy.

A wide loop brought him around the back of his neighbor's houses to a nearby church rectory where he rapped on the door.

An old sexton answered wearing a thick coat and hat, his aged face weathered and cracked like shale. Beyond him, inside the rectory, a full plate of food sat on a table. It was untouched, the same as Paul's dinner had been. Next to the table stood a rifle.

The sexton nodded. "I knew you were coming."

"It's happening tonight, the soldiers have grouped," Paul replied. "The King's army will arrive shortly. You know what to do?"

"Please, Paul, it's been playing through my mind for days. How could I forget?"

"Yes, well, I've seen you play chess . . . I can only blame senility for some of those moves."

The two men smiled at each other, an attempt to add levity to the moment.

"I will be in touch," Paul said, turning to leave.

"Paul, wait, I . . . something feels wrong."

"Yes, the enemy is coming—"

"No, I mean, there have been occurrences of late . . . ever since you got back from New Hampshire. Missing livestock, blood on the flagstones. One of the stable boys said he saw red eyes in the woods on the way to Charleston. I may have seen something myself."

"Relax. The enemy would have us afraid," replied Paul, "with trickery and deceit. But they are the ones who will know fear. I must hurry. I await your signal."

With a tip of his hat, Paul turned and headed for the river docks.

● ● ●

The sexton closed the door. The food on the table was of no more interest to him, so he took it out back and left it for the stray cats—though it had been days since he'd seen the cute creatures. Next, he took up his gun, left the rectory and entered the church. It was cold and dark and the timber groaned as he walked to the altar. The moon showed through the window at the front, painting a sallow square on the floor.

Here, the sexton prayed for Paul's safety, and prayed to quell his apprehension about what the stableboys were reporting about the missing livestock. When he was done, he took the stairs to the top of the steeple and stepped out into the open, bitter air. Close by, the sea was restless, the scent of salt heavy on the breeze. Below him, the town streets were bare. No doubt Paul had already met some locals along the way and warned them of the night's impending events; everyone would be preparing, waiting at home with guns drawn.

He looked toward the tree line, out toward where he had seen the large black shape lurking the night before. He didn't see it now. But somehow, before this night was over, he knew he would.

• • •

Paul ran, keeping to the edge of town. The side streets gave way to a cow trail that led to the river docks. There he stopped, sucking in bitter, frigid air that stung his lungs, checking to make sure he was alone. His coat was just barely keeping him warm, and where there was a piece torn out of the back of the collar, the icy wind bit into his flesh. He'd lost the swatch sometime back in December, back in New Hampshire.

His rest over, he resumed his jog down the path until the river's brine hit his nose. Then, rounding a section of the trail near the water, he ran right into a roadblock. Four men, dressed in red, carrying guns. The enemy! But they were facing the other way.

Crouching down, he found a large rock at his feet, grabbed it and pitched it into the woods. The guards' heads snapped toward the noise.

"Wha's that?" one of them asked, slowly moving toward the surrounding foliage to investigate.

"I don't like it out 'ere one bit," another answered.

"There's noises in these woods what not human. You heard what they found? They say it's here."

"I 'ear lots I choose to ignore. Just stay bloody alert."

Stepping lightly, Paul found an adjoining path, followed it down to the water. A goopy fog hovered over it like a wall of uncertainty, and nearby the bells of a ship chimed in time to the lapping waves. Paul touched his weapon. At that instant, two figures in black stepped from the trees. Paul pulled his gun and aimed.

"Helluva night, aye, Paul?" It was Joshua and Thomas, prepared as always.

"It's begun," Paul replied, breathing heavy. His heart was only beginning to slow a beat. Shouldering his gun, he said, "We have to get by the ship. Get north."

"What word of the arrival," Joshua asked as he motioned for Paul to follow him to the water's edge. On the shore sat a small boat loaded with two oars.

"We'll know as we go," Paul said, climbing into the boat.

●　●　●

To the north, near the river, the fog was thickening. Whether Paul would see the signal through such a dense barrier, the sexton wondered, was anyone's guess.

Looking back toward the south bay, searching for signs of movement, the sexton froze. At the end of a thin tree-lined street, two red eyes slipped out of the dark foliage and disappeared behind a small house. Picking up his rifle, he pointed it in the direction of the eyes, but they did not return.

"They're here!"

The cry came from the center of town. The sexton swung his rifle toward Main Street with shaking arms but lowered it when he saw the troops marching down the street. "My God," he whispered. There were several thousand of them, dressed in red, with rifles and bayonets pointing toward the sky, the faintest glimmer of moonlight playing on their blades. They marched with the tautness of a lion on the prowl, heading toward the river to cross north.

The signal, the sexton thought, I have to warn everyone! The gun dropped to the floor as he took out his matches, turned back to get the gas lamps off the small table, and came face to face with two red eyes, black slit nostrils, blood-stained fangs, and two small horns sticking out of wiry hair.

"What in the foulest depths of—"

White hot pain roared across his cheek as the creature's claws opened his face. The stinging gash was unbearable, fiery and itchy. But he dared not scream lest he alert the Regulars of the plan. Paul had to find ground in Charleston first.

With a thud, the creature leapt inside the steeple, keeping to the shadows at the edge of the walls. It was not a large steeple by any means, but enough to momentarily cause the sexton to lose the whereabouts of the monster as it walked around him. Frantically reaching for his fallen gun, he was suddenly yanked backwards by his feet.

"Demon, I've been expecting you!" the sexton spit. "May God strike you down and—"

The creature flung him into the wall, the matches scattering onto the floor like scurrying insects. The impact tore a second gash in his forehead and lit up stars behind his eyes. Providentially, he landed next to his gun and groped his hand around it. But he couldn't fire yet; the Regulars would hear a gunshot, he knew. Paul needed the signal first. The Sons needed the signal.

The creature's head slunk into a moonbeam and revealed a face like that of a giant salamander. Snarling, it bit down on the gun stock, thrashed it out of the sexton's hands, and tore it in two. Its red eyes burned, its gaping mouth leaked saliva.

Backing away, the sexton's hand played over the fallen matches and an idea sparked in him. "Spawned from hellfire? I'll show you God's fire."

The old man struck a match and tossed it at the creature's wire-thick fur. A small patch caught fire and the creature's red eyes bulged. It pressed its nose into the sexton's throat, huffed putrid breath into his face. Reeling, the old man picked up the splintered gun barrel and rammed it forward, crunching it through the creature's thick skin, dousing his arms in hot blood.

With a wail, the creature leapt over the side of the steeple, down to the ground below where it rolled to put out the flames. With an agitated chuff, it took off running. The sexton looked to see where it was headed and caught a flash of its tail as it charged into the blackness of the trees, heading north. North toward Paul.

Paul! he thought. The signal!

Grabbing up two of the lanterns, he lit them and held them high. His face blazed with searing infection, and his ribs were surely cracked. Still, he held the lamps, all the while wondering how best to warn everyone of this other threat on the loose.

● ● ●

On the far shore they pulled the small boat onto the

land. Through the night's fog, Paul was just able to make out two orange glows, like distant dying suns. Joshua saw it too and pointed. "Look! They're crossing the river, marching here."

"Yes," Paul replied. He grabbed both Thomas and Joshua's hands, shook them fervently. "Thank you. The Sons thank you, too."

"I still can't believe that ship didn't hear us," Thomas said. He raised an oar wrapped in an old petticoat. "Didn't really think this would work."

"Quiet as a sleeping baby's breath," Joshua added.

Paul left them to their own devices, and ran north into Charleston. Two vagrants picking through a feed trough betrayed the town's only silence, but they scampered down an alley when they saw Paul. The town center was also bare, most people having retired for the night. Stopping under the gas lamp outside a mercantile storefront, Paul cupped his hands to his lips and took a breath. Here was the moment they'd all been waiting for. Here is where he gave up the last of his freedom under the current rule. Let my lungs be strong, he prayed.

"The Regulars are coming!"

He ran down the street repeating it over and over: "The Regulars are coming! The Regulars are coming!" He rapped on doors, he kicked storefronts, he banged on windows. Doors opened, gas lamps lit, people emerged with children hugging their legs. Yes, they had known it would happen sooner or later. The Regulars were coming.

● ● ●

Joshua and Thomas were half way back across the river when they heard the distant cry of Paul waking the town. They spoke in glances, aware that they were nearing the *Somerset*. The large man-of-war had been anchored on the river for a month now, and was manned with the enemy. They rowed slower to lessen the noise. Joshua finally spoke: "I hear Paul. Think they can hear him, too?"

"If we can, they must—"

The boat lurched! Something smashed into the bottom, tipping it up. Both men threw their arms up to stay balanced, almost dropping the oars. It splashed down again and thankfully remained upright. There was a moment of silence and then a low splashing sound in the water, passing by them. Looking back toward Charleston, the men watched as a large wake cut across the surface of the water, heading toward Paul's screams.

"The devil was that?"

"Shh. A bluefish I reckon. Let's get home. I'm freezing."

● ● ●

"Paul, you're a dreadful sight."

Paul sat at the table of Deacon John Larkin, momentarily warming his hands, wishing he was back home without the fear he felt inside of him giving him such cramps.

"The Sons saw the signal, the lanterns, right before you arrived," Larkin continued. "The plan is working so far."

"John and Sam won't know. They'll be taken by surprise unless we warn them somehow. Lord, I'm frozen to the point of pain."

Larkin looked out his window toward the river; no sign of the Regulars yet. "You have more than a moments lead. But they'll be coming fast." He looked back at the runner, saw the flushed cheeks and heaving chest and felt the man's pain. Still, he couldn't urge Paul to stop; the detriment would be too high if John and Sam were captured. "Brown Beauty is out back. She's yours."

"Are you sure? It's a long way. Can she handle it?"

"She can handle it. She's my best. There is much to do here now. Hurry! You must go."

As Paul was leaving, Larkin gripped his shoulder. "It's up to you."

"My life for it. If necessary."

Paul found the horse behind the house, undid her reins, and climbed atop her. "I hear you are fast, girl," he cooed to her. "Fast enough to save us all, I hope."

He kicked her sides and she took off through the town. Disheveled people lined the streets, some shaking in anticipation, some shaking with fear. He yelled as he went: "The Regulars are coming!"

● ● ●

It crawled onto the land, sniffed the air. Its prey had been here recently, the stench of human sweat was only outdone by the recent defecation of some nearby doe. Oh, how it loved the smell of flesh, be it man or animal. But especially man. It moved cautiously toward the lights ahead, toward the hive, where beings stood in dim rectangle lights looking around. Too many of them, it decided, it couldn't go that way.

Heading west for a minute, it found a cow trail that put it through a darker part of the town, near the fields. It hugged the trees as it went, sniffing the air to retain the scent of its prey.

● ● ●

Brown Beauty obeyed Paul's every command, leaping boulders and zig-zagging around trees like a honey bee. She was fast, as Larkin had promised, and while she knew nothing of revolution, was keenly aware of the night's fear and tension. She was full of it now, and it drove her.

Paul kicked her sides again as the town of Medford faded into the shadows behind him, its residents awake and watching the streets now. Ahead lay the bridge to Menotomy.

• • •

The creature's chest hurt. Blood trickled from where the old human had wounded it. It felt a pang of shame at having run away, but knew it couldn't afford to be slowed down. It had its orders, after all. Better to continue on its quest than die unfulfilled. Waiting for the signal to attack had felt like an eternity. The chickens and sheep it had had to eat to stay undetected for weeks had not satiated it in any real sense. Human blood was the best opiate.

At the northern tip of Medford, it slunk out of the trees near an abandoned cobble-stoned street and spotted a dirty human digging through a trash pile. Even through the considerable distance between them, the monster could smell the harsh fumes of human waste and sweat.

Like the man, it was hungry. It was always hungry. And since it had received its signal tonight, humans were now allowed.

Built for speed by the gods, it covered the hundred yards in seconds flat. The hungry man had just a moment to hear its approach, question the noise, and turn around before the beast was in the air, swiping with its claws. The man's head exploded into chunks like an apple shot by a bullet.

• • •

The river was black, the moon hidden behind charcoal clouds, the dead land covered in fog. As Paul neared the bridge, three men in dark red coats swam into view. One of them shouted: "Halt! Identify yourself!"

"Yah!" Paul shouted, kicking Brown Beauty in the ribs. With breakneck speed, he plowed through the sentries, sending them to the ground where they scrambled to fire their weapons. The pellets whizzed by Paul's ears and struck home in the nearby trees.

"I will return the sentiment!" Paul hollered back to them as he rode off the bridge and into the woods.

A mile passed, and then another. The trail was dark and deathly frigid, the bare tree limbs looming overhead like crippled bones. At a dip in the road, Paul slowed the horse and moved her to a half-frozen puddle. "Whoa, girl. Take a drink."

The horse bent down and drank as the wind howled through the boughs. Yet, aside from the wind, the forest was strangely quiet. No scurrying rodents, no hooting owls. It was as if the creatures were afraid of something.

"Be quick about it, girl. I'm not much for ghosts but this place—"

Brown Beauty's head snapped up. Paul heard the noise too. "What is that?" It was someone on horseback, coming his way.

There was no time to hide. The enemy must have followed him from the bridge; he would have to make a stand. Unshouldering his gun, he spun Brown Beauty around and aimed into the darkness.

A horse came barreling out of the black, a figure atop it, a gun in its hand.

"I've come for you, you bastard Regular!" it shouted.

Paul relaxed, he knew the voice. "William, it's me. Paul," he yelled back.

William rode up on his horse, letting his gun face the ground. "Ah, Paul, I thought you were one of them Regular scums. So . . . they sent for you, too."

"Yes. Who else to run through the cold night? My blood is ice these days."

"Damn winter is lingering, that's for sure."

"Were you followed?"

"Ha! I'm not that obvious. Let's not forget who made it in and out of Madame Raleigh's establishment for an entire month without paying." He laughed.

Paul laughed too. "You know the route they're taking, I presume?"

"I do," William replied.

They shook hands across their steeds. "Ride with me to Lexington," Paul said. And as he said it there were faint screams from back toward the bridge. "Sounds like those bastard Regulars at the bridge are being punished by their superiors for letting us get through. We should hurry to John and Sam while we can. The cache is exposed."

"I'll race you. Let's go."

● ● ●

Its muscles were hard as bricks, propelling it forward like an arrow. Behind it, at the entrance to the bridge, three mutilated humans lay oozing fluids onto the dirt. It had fed on them for a moment, then realized its mistake. The red humans were off limits. The creature would likely be reprimanded, perhaps even punished now, unless it fulfilled its duty. No matter, between the vagrant and the sentries, the furnace in its belly had fuel for a while. It had a job to do, and the stench of its prey was not far off.

• • •

Paul and William rode into Lexington, their horses hot and chuffing. The fog still rolled along the ground, reflecting the moon whenever it slid from behind the clouds. They both shouted, "The Regulars are coming! Wake up and get ready! The Regulars are coming!"

"Where are John and Sam?" William finally asked.

Paul steered Brown Beauty toward a small house on the far side of town. It was the kind of decrepit, insignificant house even termites would overlook, purposefully chosen for its ruse. These are the tactics that have allowed the Sons of Liberty to progress, thought Paul. He dismounted and knocked on the door. A small man with gray hair answered. "Yes?"

"You know who I am?" Paul asked.

The man scratched his chin. "Yes."

From behind Paul, William stuck his head forward.

"Where are Mr. Adams and Mr. Hancock? Now, old man!"

But before the man could answer, the two men in question appeared behind him.

"Paul," Sam Adams said. He could say no more as he knew what Paul's presence meant.

"It has begun," Paul answered. "You must leave now. William and I will continue on from here, and prepare everyone."

"How much time?" The second man asked.

"Perhaps an hour, perhaps less."

● ● ●

It was getting closer, it could see lights through the ground cloud. A town was coming into focus. It slowed its run to a trot, then to a walk. People were running this way and that, a drum was being beaten. There was too much activity to approach outright. Again, it would have to maneuver around the edge of the habitat. The smell of its prey was very strong, but even so, it might have to lay in wait until it could get a clear path to the man it was after.

Slinking into the weeds, it crawled on its hairy belly to a nearby chicken coop, bit the wooden slats in half and tore at the three chickens inside before they had time to squawk. Chicken blood was foul in comparison to human blood, but it would do. Several feet away, the humans lit fires and ran about shouting.

• • •

John and Sam sat atop their horses, pointed away from Lexington. The fog had drifted further to the ground and pooled there like water. William was about pounding on doors and helping people barricade their homes.

"Thanks for coming, Paul," Sam said. "We'll send word when we reach safety."

"I will follow you out to be safe," Paul replied.

The three of them set off into the darkness while behind them William's voice rang out: "Everybody wake up! Get your guns!"

They were a few minutes out, the noise of the town disappearing steadily, when John spoke up, "What about the papers?"

Sam and John exchanged glances, stopped their horses, and then looked at Paul. "There is a trunk, in a tavern . . . if it should fall into enemy hands . . . "

"It is taken care of," Paul said. "Now go!" He slapped their horses and they bolted into the darkness.

It took but a moment to return to the town, where even more people were now out running around. Women were crying and hugging their husbands, men were loading guns; dogs barked, horses whinnied. Paul grabbed a young boy who was running by with a rifle, yanked him to a stop. The boy was afraid, his inexperience with war plainly visible in his eyes. "The Tavern?" Paul asked. "Don't stand there, boy, tell me where the tavern is!"

"Over here."

Paul grabbed two more men with guns and beckoned them to help. Together, the four of them entered the dark tavern. "Spread out and find the trunk," Paul ordered. "Don't waste time!"

The four of them stumbled around in the dark, knocking into tables and chairs, muttering curses as they banged their shins. From the back room the boy's voice called out: "Over here. I found it!"

All four men were there in a heartbeat, staring at the large trunk filled with records of the Sons of Liberty. "We must carry it out of here and arrange to get it to Mr. Hancock and Mr. Adams. Help me with it."

● ● ●

A new smell was in the air. The smell of a thousand humans from somewhere else. The beast lifted its head out of the tall weeds, the chicken blood on its nose congealed and cold, and looked toward the woods it recently came through. Visible within the criss-crossed limbs, a sea of red was marching.

Somewhere in the recesses of its eons-old brain, it knew not to bother the red humans. Somehow it knew they were off limits. It didn't know how it knew these things, it just knew.

Slinking through the grass, it moved further away from the town. Its prey was still close by, but it would have to wait even longer now.

● ● ●

"Pick it up!" Paul shouted. "We have to hurry!"

The four men struggled with the heavy trunk as they carried it up a dirt road toward the woods. If I keep exerting myself, thought Paul, I'll never last the night. I've come too far to give up now.

William appeared on horseback, leading Brown Beauty alongside by her rein. "Paul!" he shouted. "Paul! They're here!"

Paul and his workers dropped the trunk. Nobody spoke. Nobody moved. They all looked back toward the other end of town, where the morning's sun was just climbing over the horizon, not yet high enough to reveal the approaching army.

"The men are gathering on the field." William said. He was doused in mud and wet with sweat, but he was strangely calm, eager even.

"We have to get north, warn the others," Paul replied. "Quickly men, heave!"

They picked up the trunk once more and carried it uphill.

● ● ●

It was slinking around the field, staying close to the trees. Many men had gathered in the field, each holding the same type of weapon that had wounded its chest hours before. Too many men with too many weapons. The situation was growing worse. Better to get away from this threat. It moved slowly, working its way toward the north

● ● ●

The morning sun crested the horizon, spilling gold over the moist green and brown field. The air was damp and cold, the smell of birch and oak pungent. Men of varying ages, from boys to seniors, stood still as the fog swirled around their feet. A sea of red jackets marched their way, trampling the beginnings of spring's grass back to dirt. In the trees, a single bird began the first song of the morning; the last song some of the men would ever hear.

The sea of red made its way through the town, leaving a trail of cries and screams in its wake, then marched onto the field and stopped. In tiers, the enemy positioned itself for battle, the men in front dropping to their knees, the men in back pointing their guns over the heads of the front row.

Several seconds passed and nobody was sure what to do.

Then, it was a Regular who saw movement in the trees past the Rebels. Something dark and low lurking just out of view. So they want to fight dirty and sneak up on us, the man thought. With a flex of his finger, he fired at the figure in the trees, his shaking hands causing the bullet to veer at an angle and strike one of the rebel's instead.

Lead pellets cut the air and men began to fall.

• • •

Paul and William jerked at the noise. Not far away, the Battle of Lexington Green had begun. How many men will die today, Paul wondered. And do they realize what they are dying for? And a final thought: I am terrified. "You three, get the trunk to John and Sam. William,—"

"We have work yet to do. I know. Let's hurry."

Mounting Brown Beauty once more, Paul sympathized with the mare's obvious fatigue. But he was in desperate need of her agility. Should the men on the field fall to the Regulars, the next stop would be Concord, where the munitions cache lay in hiding.

The two horses pounded over the frozen ground, racing with an urgency they could not understand. The woods closed in on them as the trails narrowed and became a few single paths northward. The chill air was warming ever so slightly, but the remaining fog was still cold.

"They arrived faster than I thought," William said over the rapid hoof beats.

"Lexington will hold them for a few," Paul replied, "but they will be close behind."

"Should we find a blockade, I stand at your side. You know that."

"No, should we be blocked one of us must draw all

attention so that the other can ride on. Promise me!"

Both men agreed.

It was then a horse carrying a lanky man came barreling around a curve in the trail, narrowly missing the riders. Both men reared and up and nearly fell off their steeds. "What the hell!" shouted Paul.

The new man diverted his horse into the woods and rode behind the trees, pulling his weapon. Paul and William drew their guns and aimed but the thick lattice work of birch and maple branches offered only slivers of the man.

"There he is!" shouted William.

"Show yourself!"

"I can't get a shot."

"There!"

From out of the trees, the man suddenly appeared with his rifle aimed at Paul. All three men bared their teeth, flexed their stomach muscles. It was Paul who shouted.

"Nobody shoot!"

Everyone held their weapons out, nobody daring to move. The man on the horse broke the silence.

"Dr. Samuel Prescott," he said, "and you are?"

Paul nodded. "Paul Revere. This here is William Dawes."

"Ah. I've heard of you, Mr. Revere."

"Have you now?"

"Of course. I too am a patriot. Your name gets around."

"You damn near killed us there."

"Many apologies. I did not expect to see anyone on the road."

"You're aware the Regulars are right now fighting in Lexington. Why are you riding about?"

"I was . . . visiting . . . a friend. Something came up. It was better for me to leave."

"Ha!" exclaimed William. "I'm not dense, you know. You and your lady friend were caught with your pants down? By her husband, I assume."

The three men laughed. In the distance there was a low explosion. The horses became uneasy and walked in circles and the laughter died on the spot.

"Time for jokes later," Paul said. "We're off to Concord. I'll not have these Regular scum taking our stores."

"Concord, huh?" Prescott rubbed his chin. "Well I'm not welcome in Lexington, that's for sure. But I'm headed to Concord myself."

"What for?"

"Hell, I live there. And I can tell you now, the site of you two riding into town covered in mud and smoke would scare the devil. You're likely to get shot like that. They know me there. Let me come with you."

"You might want to rethink—"

"Rethink what? Because you are wanted men? I told you, I'm a patriot too. This is revolution and I offer my services for it."

William reined in his horse, kicked its side. "You do take risks, don't you, doctor?"

The three men headed north through the woods.

● ● ●

The beast ran at full tilt, the warm morning air renewing its strength. It knew the man in red on the battlefield had tried to shoot it, and so it was best to get away quickly. Its chest was slowly beginning to heal, but it was getting hungry again. There were hoofprints on the ground, fresh ones, leading to the north. Its prey was riding with companions. No matter, it would take them all out, shred their skin and feast on their viscera. It had been promised rewards, possibly even more human flesh, possibly the chance to remain in this world for good. Its master was harsh, a man with a soul blacker than the beast's gums, but he was fair.

The creature found a reserve of energy and bounded forward.

● ● ●

A small house sat on the side of a hill, not far from Lincoln. There was no light inside it, and no sign of life save for a small cat sleeping near the door.

The three riders approached it. They were about to descend their horses and knock on the door to warn the remote inhabitant of the coming threat, when a voice rang out behind them.

"Halt!"

The men spun around.

A small group of Regulars on horseback were aiming their guns at them. They must have been watching us the whole while, Paul thought. They snuck up on us.

"Ride through!" Paul shouted.

The group of Regulars rode directly at Paul and his companions. Both parties crashed into each other, the horrific scream of injured horses and terrified men echoing through the dew-covered woods.

Fists flew, a gun was fired, a horse toppled. Swinging the butt of his rifle, Samuel clipped one of the enemy on the chin and knocked him off his horse. William was engaged in a headlock fight. A bayonet flashed and tore at Paul's jacket, tearing off a hole above where he'd lost the other piece back in December.

Both sides bit and punched and kicked.

Samuel got off another swing and freed William from his captor. The two men fought to get to Paul, who was wrestling a bayonet-tipped rifle away from one of the Regulars. But they were pushed back.

"Forget it, Samuel! Let's go!"

"But Paul—"

"Will be angry if we don't leave. Come on!"

William grabbed Samuel's horse and yanked it away from the struggle. The two men bounded through the forest, with two Regulars in pursuit.

● ● ●

It was over in minutes. Paul sat on the ground, his

hands splayed out to his sides, a gun at his head. "Where are you headed?" the British captain asked him.

Paul answered, "To rouse your demise. Go on and kill me, it'll serve you no good. I've alrcady awakened half the land and warned them."

"Have you now? Well, I dare say that your efforts have been in vain."

"We have a militia twice the size of your army. You'd do well to return to your cages overseas."

A smaller soldier smacked Paul across the back of the head. "Let's just be done with him now."

"I'm not finished," the captain said. Then to Paul: "Where is the munitions cache? We know it's in Concord. Tell me where."

"Ride to Concord and find it yourself," Paul spit, "if you can get through our men."

The two soldiers who had raced after William and Samuel on horseback returned. One of them was pulling William's horse behind his own. "They got away, split up. But one is on foot so I don't think he'll be a problem."

"The other?" The captain asked.

"Over a rock wall, through the thickets. We couldn't keep up. Must be a local, he knew exactly where to go. We lost him in the trees."

The captain removed his gun from Paul's head, took a moment to look around, walked to the soldier holding William's horse. The morning fog was all but gone, the insects now showing signs of life. The birds were signing joyously, ignorant of the coming bloodshed.

Brown Beauty, being held by yet another soldier, sniffed the grass.

The men began conversing in whispers. Paul could only hear bits and pieces: "If it's true we're in trouble . . . half the countryside . . . miles to Concord . . . .they might be waiting for us . . . but we have a weapon . . . it's not a rumor, I heard from a confidant . . . witchcraft they say . . . found him in Dorchester in a cave . . . very powerful they say . . . I'll take my chances . . . "

The captain returned, bent down and looked in Paul's face. Behind him the horses became unruly, Brown Beauty tugging at her reins. The birds stopped singing.

"Your tales of a militia may be true, but we have powerful weapons too. Strange, yet powerful ones. So, if you're not going to tell us where the munitions cache is, then I have no further use for you."

He placed his gun against Paul's head. Before he could pull the trigger something growled and his arm fell in a bloody heap to the ground.

● ● ●

It was salivating. This was its prey. It was so overcome with hunger and joy it didn't care if the red humans were off limits or not. It inched slowly through the tall grass, watching the horses and men. It wanted its kill, and this other human was interfering. Taking its prey from it. With lighting reflexes, it lashed out with its razor sharp claws and took the interfering human's arm off.

There were screams, there was blood, it was hungry, this was its prey.

Now it would feast.

● ● ●

" . . . the bloody hell is that!"

The soldiers fired, but in their terrified state completely missed the beast. It leapt up and sliced the senior soldier's head off. Bounding off the torso onto the nearby horse, it bit the ribcage out of the man holding the rein. It turned and bared its teeth, let everyone see its red eyes and horns, wiry hair and brown scales and salamander body, let them know it was from another world.

"The devil!" somebody screamed. The remaining Regulars took off running and screaming.

Paul was up in a flash, on top of Brown Beauty. His gun was a ways off. No time to get it. He kicked the horse and rode away.

● ● ●

The beast watched him go, taking an extra moment to bite the lower jaw off the last horseman. For good measure, it tore the horses' throats with a quick swipe of its claws. Then it headed after Paul.

● ● ●

"Ride, girl, ride!" Paul shouted. What the devil was that beast? It was certainly no animal. It was something else. It had horns, it had blood red eyes, its claws were sharper than swords.

The beast's heavy breath grew louder and louder behind him. It was chasing him and gaining!

Paul spun around in the saddle and caught sight of the beast speeding down the trail toward him. It was so fast! It darted into the trees and leapt over logs and rocks with the agility of a deer, puffing through remaining patches of morning fog. Within seconds it was running alongside him.

Paul yanked Brown Beauty to the side. The horse slammed into a tree and spun around like a tornado, let out a guttural wail, and landed on its side in the dirt. Paul went flying into the brush, rolled himself up to his feet as white-hot pain blazed up his side. He snapped a sabre-length limb off the nearest tree. Something wet ran down his side but he dared not look.

The beast was on the horse before Paul was fully upright, tearing the animal's insides out and jamming its face down into the newly-opened hole. When it lifted its head, the horse's heart was in its teeth.

Standing motionless, Paul watched the beast drop the heart, as if it had more pressing business. It cocked its head and stared at him, bared its blood-stained teeth. Was that recognition in its eyes? Did it know who Paul was?

Paul hefted the limb.

The beast leapt.

With all his might, Paul swung the branch and caught the monster in mid air. The limb broke in two and the beast landed on top of him, snapping at his neck. Without hesitation, Paul rammed the remaining piece of limb into its mouth, driving it straight down its throat until there was a sickening crunch.

The beast leapt back with the limb sticking out of its mouth, frantically shook its head to dislodge it, finally trying to yank it out with its claws. But it was stuck fast and the beast rolled on the ground in pain and discomfort, choking and gagging.

"What the hell are you?"

Paul didn't wait for an answer. He grabbed his side and ran through the woods, back toward the house in the field. As he ran, the creature's coughs and growls rang through the woods, a pained howling unlike anything from this earth.

It took several minutes to get back to the house where dead Regulars lay in various states of mutilation on the brown grass. Paul found his gun, along with the Regulars' weapons, snatched them up and pounded on the door of the house. Still nobody answered, so he kicked it open

No sooner did he shut it than the beast was charging at the door, the limb free of its mouth. Blood streaked its cheek like war paint. It slammed against the door, knocking dirt loose from the ceiling. Paul threw his back to it to keep it shut and the impact nearly knocked him to the ground. The house was mostly bare, full of dust and cobwebs. Each wall contained a window through which the morning sun shined, dust motes dancing in the rays. It could come through any of the windows, Paul thought.

"What do you want with me!"

It continued to crash against the door, shaking the house, but then as quickly as it came, it stopped.

There was so much adrenaline coursing through Paul he could not breathe slow enough to move without coughing. Where was the damned creature? He spun frantically from window to window but could not see it, though he heard birds taking flight outside.

The momentary silence that followed was elongated by the thumping sounds of his own heart. Secret weapon, he thought, remembering the words the Regular had used. Is this their secret weapon?

It crashed through the window next to the door, glass shards shooting through the air. Paul swung the gun in his right hand and fired. It was empty! The beast landed awkwardly and stumbled, was on its side on the floor, attempting to right itself, slipping on the shards.

He fired the gun in his left, his own gun, but the beast was already in the air and the bullet struck the far wall. He only had a moment to take in the salamander-like head before both beast and man rolled on the floor, into the open fireplace. An old vase, cracked and gray with dust, fell off the mantle and shattered. Paul grabbed the nearest shard, drove it into the beast's eye and screamed. Razor teeth tore at his arm, sank in near the elbow as he punched the beast in the other eye, momentarily blinding it.

Scrambling out from under it, Paul found the gun and stabbed the bayonet into the creature's back. The creature shook to dislodge the knife and the glass shard, lashed out with its claw, missed Paul and tore a chunk out of the wall.

Paul fell back, landed on his rear with a thud. Blood ran freely from his arm and his side, and his adrenaline was wearing off. Moving pained every part of his body. "All right then, have at me. I've done my job, I am prepared!"

The creature moved forward, a bit slower than before. Its wounds were obvious, but it was still strong. A smell like wet leaves emanated from it, a gooey yellow mucus ran down from its eyes. Its throat was swollen, its chest was torn. It radiated heat, and it was determined to have its meal. With a final roar, it charged at Paul.

"Our father, who art—"

A shot rang out; a bullet shattered the far window. Slick blood sprayed into Paul's face as the beast slammed into him, dragging him across the floor underneath its body, before coming to rest against the wall. Its face lay on Paul's own, its red eyes staring through him, the bullet hole in its head gushing blood. Slowly, its tongue fell out and flopped on Paul's neck, dribbled saliva down his shoulder.

On the verge of tears, Paul fought to control his mind. Whatever it was, it had meant to kill him, and only him, as if he were the choicest cut of meat in the land. There was recognition in its eyes even now. He couldn't speak, and his heart began to ache from beating so fast. How does it know me, he wondered. What have I done?

As he watched, the creature's eyes drained of color, moving from red to pink to gray. And he saw they were not demon eyes, they were human eyes. "What are you?" Paul asked again.

Then slowly, the eyes glazed over and all was still, except the sound of someone running toward the house.

"Paul! Paul are you all right?"

Tired, sapped of all energy, and in blistering pain, Paul rolled the beast off of him. The door opened, and a man entered, a rifle in his hand. "Paul. Thank goodness I found you. I'm not such a good shot but I think the Lord saw fit to extend a hand this time."

Paul smiled as his friend the sexton entered the home, his head covered in sweat and his face lacerated. "How did you know?" Paul asked.

Pointing to his own face, the man said, "You don't think I did this myself, do you?"

The old man helped Paul to his feet, and together they stared at the creature. "It tried to kill me," the old man said, "but then it left. I followed it to warn people, found a dead man in Medford, some dead chickens, I knew it was heading north. It didn't make much sense at first, until I remembered what you said, that the Regulars would have us afraid."

"You think this . . . thing . . . belongs to them?" Secret Weapon, thought Paul.

"I'm not sure, but it's odd that it should appear on this night and head north after you did. Some of the Regulars who fell at Lexington talked about secret weapons, dark magic, before they died."

"The Regulars? They fell?"

"They did." The old man smiled. "They retreated. It was your ride that prepared our militias. Others have already headed north, to await further battle. Paul, you have saved us. You were right, victory will be ours."

"Look!' Paul shouted, and pointed at the beast.

The creature was melting away before their eyes. Its hair dried up and became dust, its bones shrank into tiny tree branches, its blood ran across the wooden floor and evaporated, fat and viscera bubbled and burned away, its eyes popped and smoked. When it was done, only a black spot remained on the floor.

"Look at that. No one will believe us," Paul said.

"But we know. And we must be alert for more. The Regulars have something evil in their possession. And it knows who we are."

Paul nodded. "Time to go."

"We can get another horse in Lexington. I'll follow you back."

Together, the two men, both cut and bruised, rode back to Boston, keeping a lookout for strange shapes, listening to make sure the forest creatures were still stirring. From somewhere far away, the cries of battle filled the air. It was the cry of freedom.

● ● ●

"I can summon more," the old man said as he coughed and rubbed his head. "But I am old and the possession is harder to control. It wants to eat whatever it sees."

The *Sommerset* was crammed with British troops awaiting orders and crates full of weapons and food. It was hot and smelled of stale skin despite the cool breezes blowing across the water outside. The elderly man lay in a small bed, a candle beside him, sweat glistening on his face.

At the bedside, William Hearthmill, General of the king's second infantry regiment, turned away in disgust, looked at his aide. "Reports?"

"We were turned back at Lexington. This Revere awakened the countryside and they amassed before we could surprise them. Hancock and Adams slipped away."

The general drew his sword. "Pity you are the last of your kind, old man, we might have still used your services were you younger. But your monster failed. And you failed. And now we have a war to deal with. Pity. It would have been a formidable ally for us."

The old man wheezed. "You should have let me do it earlier."

"And alert the town? You old fool."

"We had him in New Hampshire."

"You swiped at him when he was surrounded by twenty men. You were a fool to even try it then. You told me your conjured beast could follow him to the leaders. And then kill them in secret. It did neither."

"I can try again. I can summon another."

"I think not. This time we will fight man to man. It is a small collection of provinces, the people are inept and have no proper military of their own. We will crush them. When you see your monster in hell, say hello to it for me."

"But . . . " the old man raised his hand.

"Goodbye." The general thrust his sword through the man's throat, killing him instantly. Then, to his aide, "Gather the troops, and get me some ink. I will inform His Majesty we need more troops. And then we will crush this ridiculous collection of infidels. No more magic, no more old wizards. The old ways are dead. Victory will be ours by our hands alone."

ONE OF THESE DAYS

WHEN I GOT out of the shower, I found Thomas sitting on my couch watching TV and drinking a cup of coffee. For a lawyer, he was always nervous, and today was no exception. His hands were shaking so badly coffee was spilling onto his thousand-dollar suit; the suit he afforded from the *per diem* I provided him. But then, he was worth it, had never lost a case. And I'd had plenty.

"Remind me to take your key away," I said to him as I made my way to the kitchen to pour a cup for my-self.

"I couldn't sleep last night," he said, "kept tossing and turning. I figured I'd meet you. I knocked but . . . um . . . the maid didn't . . . anyway, I made coffee."

As I passed by the TV, I saw a newscast from Japan. An angry mob was holding up signs and yelling into the camera. The protesting was so loud that the anchorman was cupping his earpiece and shouting at the top of his lungs to be heard. Not that it mattered any-way, neither Thomas nor I could understand Japanese.

Before I could tell Thomas to change the channel, the image switched to a young news reporter standing in Tiergarten Park in Germany. It was the same type of scene, just different scenery.

"Turn that off," I told him, "put on some cartoons or something."

"There aren't any cartoons on this morning. The

coverage is everywhere."

"Well, throw a DVD in or something."

Reluctantly, Thomas stood and put in a Bugs Bunny DVD and came into the kitchen. He stood against the wall, leaning on my Marvel Comics calendar, while I poured my drink.

"You know, you can still back out," he said. "People might forgive—"

"No. No backing out. It's my decision and I'm carrying through. Do you have a problem with that?"

His shaking hands betrayed his words. "Of course not. Why would I have a problem? It's just, you know, as your lawyer I'm obligated to tell you about...I just want you to know all your options."

"I know my options. Hand me the sugar bowl."

From outside came the sound of a car engine. Checking my watch, I realized that my driver, Santino, was pulling the Rolls into the driveway. He was right on time as usual. Thomas read my mind, frowned and said, "Then I guess we should go get this over with."

"Don't give me that look, Thomas. This should have been done ages ago." I drank the coffee, got dressed, and left with Thomas in tow.

● ● ●

My Rolls is a vintage 1930 Limousine Cockshoot purchased from an antique dealer in Prague. I paid extra to have it airlifted in a cargo plane because I didn't trust shipping it on a barge; cargo containers are not hermetic and the salty air of the sea will destroy a car's body. It is a very rare automobile, which is why the Rolls Royce Enthusiasts Club in my state keeps pushing for me to join. But I want nothing to do with them.

Thomas and I sat in the back while Santino drove. The radio was buzzing with news reporters yelling my name so I had Santino put in a Hank Williams CD. The morning paper was on the seat next to me, my face covering the front page, so I flipped it over.

About twenty minutes away from my estate, on the main highway, we slowed to a stop. "Senor," Santino said, looking at me in the rear view mirror, "there is a traffic jam. Should I take the 357 and go north?"

Looking out the front window, I saw hundreds of cars trying desperately to get around one another but not going anywhere. More than a few were crashed together, their owners standing on the sides of the road waving their hands like grandstand conductors. Thomas gulped and suggested I take Santino's advice.

"That won't be necessary," I said. I waved my hand toward the cars and they all flew off the road and hurtled several yards into the hills on either side. Car horns erupted all around as people ran screaming away from the freeway. More than a few men pointed at my Rolls and made the sign of the Devil.

Santino didn't say a word, but Thomas registered his own disdain for my actions by looking out the window. It mattered little to me, and he knew it. I had learned a long time ago that the lawyer was not really my friend, and didn't care about my legal security; he was simply afraid of me.

"Go ahead, Santino," I said, "the road's clear now. We should be there in fifteen minutes."

● ● ●

Indeed, we were at the park right at 9:30am, greeted by what must have been several million people waving signs and screaming obscenities. The sound was cacophonous. I could break them all in half very easily if I wanted to, could scatter them with a mere thought, but I decided against it. Perhaps when I was done with the morning's business I would teach them a lesson. Maybe pop them like beans in a microwave, or melt them like candle wax. It seemed every couple of months I had to teach the people a lesson. My periods of quiet only made them wonder if I had lost my powers, and the surest way to show them I was still godly was to give them an act of god.

Oh, I don't use the capital G for myself—I am not God—but I am something akin to a deity. Doctors and psychiatrists never could discover how or where I got my powers, but then, I'm not too concerned about it. When you can manipulate, create and destroy all matter around you with only your thoughts, you tend to just go with the flow.

Angry as the crowd was, when it saw my Rolls, it parted like the Red Sea. Cliché intended.

"That's a formidable mob," Thomas said, looking back at me again. "You know you can still—"

"Thomas, you're getting on my nerves this morning."

That shut him up. We rolled to a stop in the center of the park and got out of the car.

In the middle of the park stood a rocket ship, larger than the tallest building on earth. So large it had given me a headache just to create it. It was silver and red and looked like a giant bullet. I don't know where I got the design from, probably a comic book from my youth, but it was strangely familiar nonetheless. I knew it would fly, that was not a problem. I knew it would fly because I would make it fly. I would make them all fly, all the rockets in all the cities all over the world. All the rockets I had created over the past week. Thousands of them, each one larger than anything that had ever been constructed.

In front of the rocketship was a raised dais, and on the dais was a microphone. Ascending the steps, I reached out and tapped the microphone, happy to see it was already on. News cameras swarmed around me, flash bulbs popping. The irate crowd, still waving their signs, began to quiet down.

"Gentlemen," I said to the millions of nervous and angry men who had come to yell at me. "I see you are very angry with me, but I must ask that your emotions not rile you too much, or I will be forced to maintain peace. Let me just start the ceremony by saying, trust me, things will be better from now on."

Angry susurrations swam through the crowd.

A voice came from behind me: "Dear God, this is a mistake."

Turning away from the mic, I found Thomas standing there. "What did you say?" I asked him, *sotto voce.*

"You can't just do this because she broke up with you. It's insane."

"No, Thomas, I'll tell you what's insane—that I didn't get a new lawyer the moment you first questioned my decision. Perhaps you should tell me why I need to keep you around anymore. You're just like her . . . like everyone . . . all against me."

"She left you, Ernie, because . . . because you're insane. You treated her like garbage. She only stayed with you as long as she did because she was afraid of you. And when she didn't care anymore, she reciprocated. Can you blame her?"

"She's a bitch. They're all bitches."

"You say that because you still love her," Thomas said.

"So what if I do? I'm tired of these women thinking they can drive men crazy and we're just supposed to accept it. We're all better off without them."

"You just don't understand them is all, and for all your powers, you hate that you can't figure them out. But you know what, none of us can, and that's what's so great about them all. What will this prove? Huh? Ernie, my sister is in that ship. Does that mean anything to you?"

"No. And I'm tired of your complaining. You know

what? I think a demonstration of my powers is in order." I turned back to the microphone. "Gentlemen of Earth," (the news coverage was being aired live around the globe) "before we get started, a quick reminder of what happens to troublemakers in my midst."

I waved my hand at Thomas and his head exploded. The corpse of my former lawyer stood still for a heartbeat, then toppled over next to my feet. The crowd grew quiet at this.

"Gross, isn't it." Nobody laughed at my attempt for humor, so I decided to get on with it. "Okay then. Well, I guess this is it. Like my father always said: If it has tits or an engine it'll give you nothing but problems. Boy was he right. I know you're all a little upset now, but you'll see, in a few months, this planet will be quiet, productive, and free of decorative hand towels. You'll be able to lounge in your underwear and watch football without a single nag. You'll see, you'll thank me in no time."

I turned and looked at the giant rocketship, looked through the tiny portholes in the hull. Inside, I saw long blonde hair, high-heeled shoes, hands holding purses, lips painted red with lipstick. Millions of women, jampacked inside like dirty clothes in an overstuffed suitcase. If you listened hard you could hear their cries, which to some extent, was music to my ears.

Through one of the portholes I could see *her,* Jessica, the woman who'd broken my heart. She made eye contact with me, but all I saw there was her hatred of me.

So be it. If she didn't want me, she'd have nobody.

"Don't worry," I told the crowd. "NASA says they'll have a space station built on the moon somctimc in the next fifty years. You can see your women then. If you still want to."

With that, I waved my hand at the rocket. It rose into the sky and shot into the heavens, headed for the moon. The crowd stood gaping in disbelief, eyes locked on the myriad white contrail streaks that suddenly appeared everywhere in the sky as rockets from every city on Earth headed to the moon, each full of the one thing I would never understand: women.

MARTIN'S JOB

THERE WAS A low rumble, somewhere distant, followed by firecracker gunshots and faint screams. As if in response, the police precinct trembled, dust snowing from the ceiling. Martin held his head in his hands, stared down at the nicked interrogation table in front of him. Someone had etched *smells like bacon in here* into the surface. Elsewhere on the table, dark brown stains suggested something beyond verbal coercion, something Martin thought was only a cheap device used in television dramas.

Across the table from him, fists balled so tightly the white bone underneath looked like it was going to rip through, officer Burke loomed like a golem frozen in time. His wide jaw moved ever so slightly, chewing over possible ways to get Martin to tell the truth. It seemed he had aged ten years since the interrogation began some thirty-five minutes ago. Twice he had stepped out of the room into the bullpen, the maze of desks visible to Martin through a thick pane of Plexiglas, and asked, "Has anyone gotten hold of my wife yet?" Each time the reply was no.

Martin didn't know the joys of marriage, but still, he felt bad for the man.

Burke's eyes flicked to the solitary window in the corner of the room that looked out over the city street, stayed there for a minute, and then returned to Martin. The Herculean cop was silent, furious, scared. His attempt to hide his vulnerability wasn't fooling Martin. And that scared Martin even more. After all, Burke was authority, he was the law, he had no reason to be scared; people didn't mess with big cops.

But then, people weren't the important part of the situation unfolding around them.

Burke stopped leaning on the table and rolled his sleeves up. Faded military tattoos hid beneath wiry, dark hair. One of them was a Marine Corp logo.

"I don't know," Martin stammered. It was more an effort to fill the silence than anything else.

Out in the precinct's offices, cops ran around like excited ants. Nobody seemed to know what to do or who to call. It was chaos.

The building lurched again, the grout in the green tile walls cracking like varicose veins.

"Tell me once again about the door," Burke said.

Martin met the man's eyes. "What's to tell. It was just a door. Typical, red, with a gold knob."

"And the man who went into it?"

"Please can I go home? I don't know anything. My dog is still outside and I . . . I just want to go home."

Burke came around the table and leaned in close to Martin's face, his large head eclipsing the room's overhead light. His bloodshot eyes hovered in the shadow between them. Martin had to look away again.

"I'm trying to understand. You said there was a man, so describe him. Again."

Martin swallowed, tasted adrenaline and fear. Just thinking of the man made him afraid, as if mentioning him would bring swift retribution of some sort. "Long neck, blond hair, glasses," Martin replied. "I've already given a description. Can I have a cigarette?"

"No. This blond guy was the guy who hired you?"

Martin felt the building rumble once more, saw the overhead light swaying, heard the now familiar sound of gunshots a few streets away. He wished Burke would back off; it wasn't really his fault after all. He couldn't be held accountable. Could he?

"Yes," Martin said. "The name of the firm is—"

"We checked. Right before the Web went down. We checked. There's no such firm as Plato Processing. It doesn't exist."

"You don't believe me?"

"I'm trying."

"Well he said that's who he worked for and that's the name that was in the listing." Martin remembered the ad in the paper: *Data processor needed, part time, good pay, first come first serve. Plato Processing.*

He remembered it, but he wished he could forget.

● ● ●

The ad contained an address to an old warehouse near the shipyard. Martin rushed out there in his baby blue Taurus, the fan belt squeaking the whole way, praying he'd be the first to arrive because he was so mired down in late fees on his credit cards his only other option for getting ahead at this point would be filing bankruptcy. He smoked a Camel as he drove but it did little to relieve his stress. The nearly empty cigarette pack in his shirt pocket, purchased after scrounging change from under couch cushions, was just another reminder of his destitution.

He rehearsed answers to possible interview questions on the way, many of them lies; the resume on the seat beside him was already full of them. He needed to do whatever he could to get the job.

It was nine o'clock when he pulled into the parking lot of the warehouse. The building's façade was covered in rust and illegible graffiti. The lot was empty.

A note hung on a large metal door at the front of the building: APPLICANTS PLEASE KNOCK. He pulled his old college blazer across his neck to fight off the wind blowing off the water. Near the dock, a blackened barge rolled in the tide, a slick, dark liquid running out of a bilge hole into the water.

The door opened a crack and stopped, the occupant inside studying Martin. Then it swiftly opened wide to reveal a skinny blond man in a red knit sweater and tortoise-shell glasses. Martin immediately noticed the length of the man's neck but composed himself not to stare. He himself had grown up with a large gap in his front teeth and knew well the discomfort that came from being scrutinized over physical abnormalities.

"I'm here about the job."

"Yes. Right this way." The man motioned Martin inside and led him through the dark warehouse, past broken-down forklifts, oil drums devoured by rust, through looming shelves stacked with dusty boxes long forgotten, down a set of stairs to the basement where cobwebs were thick and unsettling. A dim bulb threw coffee-stained light onto rundown machinery.

"Just a little further," the man said. He did not smile nor seem to be embarrassed by the poor condition of the place.

They entered a long hallway littered with scraps of yellowed paper and torn cardboard boxes. Someone had smashed the glass to the fire extinguisher box on the wall and taken the extinguisher. Overhead florescent lights flickered continuously as they made their way to an office with wood paneling and an orange shag rug. A Budweiser calendar a decade old still hung on the wall. The lighting in the office was also dim, but at least it didn't flicker.

"Here's the computer you'll be working on." The man tapped the keyboard to bring the old computer out of sleep mode.

"Please." The man pulled out the desk chair.

Martin eased in behind the industrial gunmetal desk, just like the one his father used to keep in the garage growing up, and looked at the computer screen. There was a database on it filled with various names. No addresses, or telephone numbers, or additional information of any kind, just names.

"I trust you've used this program before," the man asked. His long neck was bent at a very unatural angle. Martin looked away quickly, reminding himself that dirty environments and strange staff made no difference as long as he got a paycheck. His bills were too many to be choosy.

"Yes, I've used it a bunch. Not too great with formulas but I—"

"No need for formulas. Just enter the names into the database as you get them. Last names first. Full middle names if there are any. Understand?"

Martin nodded, risked a look at the man's neck, saw that it was it bending in a new direction. It seemed to undulate ever so slightly, like a snake slithering.

His palms began to sweat, something that always happened when he felt confused and uneasy. He wiped them on his pants, realizing there were no other workers in the building. Why such a large building for such a small job? Why no interview questions? Why just names? He hadn't even told anyone where he was going. Maybe it would be best to say he forgot something in the car and leave.

"Did you have a big turnout? For the job?"

"You are first. So it's yours if you want it. It pays thirteen dollars an hour. I can pay you in full at the end of each day with cash. That way you won't have to worry about taxes."

Martin considered this. Coming home every day with pay would certainly help with the bills, especially not having to give any of it to Uncle Sam.

"That sounds great," he replied. "Will I be the only one here?"

"Yes. For now. The . . . company . . . I represent has

experienced a buildup, a spike if you will, of data, and can no longer keep track of it on their own. I realize it's not the most pleasant environment, but it was the best I could do on such short notice."

"How big a buildup?"

"We are unsure. The job might last several weeks, perhaps even slide into something more permanent . . . providing my employer sees your benefit."

"Permanent?"

"Yes, times are . . . changing. The names accumulate more rapidly than ever before. People are desperate."

Martin was lost. "And the names are—"

"Prospects. People we are keeping an eye on, though many of them we won't see for some time. Nothing illegal, I assure you."

"Oh." Martin looked at the screen, studied the names. They meant nothing to him, just random names that may as well have been numbers. Simple names like Thomas Jennifer above and below elaborate ones like Farazella Alejandro Miguel Guillermo.

"Here." The blond man tapped a stack of papers next to the computer. It was a list of names written out in long hand, though written was an understatement. They were scribed in some type of calligraphy. Though calligraphy wasn't right either. More like the fonts he'd seen on horror movie posters and heavy metal album covers: artistic and sharp, dark and ominous. It seemed a waste of time for them to be written in such a manner if all he was doing was typing them into a database.

They made his palms sweat again.

"Just go down the list and enter the names," the blond man said. "I will bring more as they come. Is everything clear?"

Martin said yes, swallowed his anxiety and thought of a daily income, how good it would feel to be back on his feet once again. With the under-the-table scale, he may as well be making almost twenty dollars an hour, not bad at all.

"Good." The long-necked man smiled and moved to a door in the back of the office. It was dark red with a gold doorknob. A small black symbol resembling a ram was painted in the center of it. Martin hadn't noticed the door before; in fact, he was pretty sure it hadn't been there when he'd entered. But then, the lights were pretty dim so he assumed he'd just missed it. The blond man stuck his finger in his sweater's collar and scratched at his neck, which continued to ripple grotesquely.

"Feel free to use the bathroom located down the hall, and to take a lunch break around noon. If you need anything, just call me at extension zero. My name is Horris."

"Sure," Martin replied.

"But please, do not open this door. No matter what you hear, it is against company policy for unauthorized personnel to open it."

And with that, the man opened the door and stepped inside. It shut behind him with a click. Martin was alone. With the door.

No matter what you hear . . .
What the hell did that mean?

• • •

The police station bucked violently. Tiles shook loose from the walls. Paperweights and phones danced off of desks. Burke moved his hand to his gun, an instinctual gesture for a career cop. Sweat dripped from his forehead and plopped on the table, mixing with the dark brown stains.

"And you opened the door," he said. "Why?"

Martin rubbed his hands together, his slick palms sliding back and forth. "I told you this too. I don't see how—"

"I know what you told me. I've been a cop for twenty years, Martin, and one thing I know sure as flies like shit is that what someone tells me happened and what actually did are never the same. So you opened the door, despite warnings not to. Why?"

Martin turned and looked out the window. Screams rose from the streets, curdled, angry, pleading with God. Car horns bleat like sheep in a slaughter house. Gunshots had gone from random pops to a constant tattoo.

"I heard something, or someone, I think."

"Heard what? Hurry up and get to it, Martin."

"A voice. Pleading. 'Let me out. Help me.' Like that."

"Man? Woman?" The cop's eyes kept flicking to the window. Seismic activity continued to shake the interrogation table.

"Man, I think. Just kept begging me to let him out, that he was being held prisoner. How could I know?"

● ● ●

Martin decided he would take a break in fifteen minutes, use the bathroom and maybe go out and have a smoke. With money guaranteed at the day's end, he could finally stop rationing his Camels. The past two hours had been dull, alone in the office entering names into the database with no one to talk to but Miss Budweiser. His wrists were starting to cramp up.

He looked at the list and found the next name. Carlos—

Boom boom! The red door erupted in a fit of banging. Someone pounded on it from the other side, someone desperate to get through. Martin jumped up and knocked the stack of papers onto the floor. His heart went from 0 to 100, slamming against his ribs. His testicles drove up into his stomach.

"Horris?" His body shook from the scare. There was no answer.

Boom boom!

The pounding was so violent Martin thought the door would explode in a hail of splinters. Frozen as he was in shock, he knew it was in his best interest to find Horris.

He picked up the phone and stabbed a finger at the zero. That's when the door stopped banging. A voice from the other side whispered, "Help me. Please don't call Horris. Help me. I'm in pain." The voice was masculine. Yet is somehow sounded wet.

Martin stood with the phone receiver against his ear, the stack of papers littered on the floor. What should he do? "Are you okay?" Stupid, Martin, he chided himself, does he sound okay? "Um . . . I'm just going to call Horris and tell him you need some help, okay?"

"NO! NO! Please don't call Horris. I need to get out, before he discovers I've left. Please help me. I'm in so much pain."

"What kind of pain?" Martin's hand hovered over the phone buttons.

The door banged again, shaking the walls. "Don't you get it! He's trapped me here. He hurts me when no one is around. I need to get out and get away or he'll keep hurting me."

"Who? Who is hurting you?"

The voice grew raspy and labored, as if running on dying batteries. "Horris. Horris is not what you think. Did you see his neck? He's not what you think. Please let me out or he will kill me."

Could this be some kind of test, Martin wondered. It seemed too surreal not to be. What purpose would such a macabre test prove?

"You saw his neck," the voice rasped, "saw it moving. You must believe me or he will get you too. That's what he does, lures people here and collects them. Right now he's preparing to come back and hit you over the head. Then he will put you in a dark room and stick things in you until he's bored. Then he will do it again and again and again. You must hurry. Please, I'm dying." The voice faded into a wheeze.

Martin had heard enough. He knew there was something way off about Horris, something his instinct was telling him not to trust, and this confirmed it. He hadn't thought it would involve people locked up in basements, but he knew it was something. Screw the money, he thought, screw this job, I need to get out of here.

"Pleeeeaase," the voice moaned.

Martin put the phone back, walked to the door. "Okay," he said. The lock for the door was on this side. He turned it, grabbed the knob. It turned easily with a faint click. As he opened the door, the phone rang, the lights flickered, and from somewhere close by Horris yelled, "Don't!"

● ● ●

Burke was staring out the window, chewing on his lips and breathing rapidly. He spun back and glared at Martin with hateful eyes. "And whatever was on the other side came out. You let it out. What was it?"

The building shifted sideways as something enormous slammed into it. Both Martin and Burke fell to the ground. Chairs flew into the walls and the interrogation table flipped over and landed on its side. Someone out in the bullpen screamed bloody murder. A gunshot, fired in panic, rang out and hit the bulletproof Plexiglas. Then, whatever had hit the building was gone, moving down the street, setting off car alarms, tearing down building facades, gouging into the road and bursting the pipes underneath. Martin didn't see any of this, but he could feel it.

Burke yanked Martin to his feet, sat him down in one of the twisted chairs. "What! Came! Out!"

"I dunno," Martin replied. "It was . . . it was...something rushed past me, something large and wet and . . . the smell made me puke. All over the floor. And when I looked up again, they were getting out of the building."

"Who? What? Tell me."

"I don't know."

"Where was the blond man?"

"He ran into the room, he tried to close the door. He was—" Martin saw it in his mind, as it replayed in a short loop. The blond man rushing in, his neck whipping about like a ribbon in the wind, his eyes pure white without pupils.

"What did I tell you, Martin?" he'd said. "I said not to open the door. Do you know how long it will take me to get them back in? Eons."

From the door, maggots the size of a cows slithered out, one after another, each with the faintest hint of a human face, each smiling and whispering *freedom freedom freedom to eat eat eat*. Past Horris and Martin they slithered, up the stairs and out towards the mid-afternoon sun. As they went they grew larger and larger, taking out doorframes and bulging the hallway's walls.

"Your inability to trust has just cost mankind its life," Horris said, his neck whipping to and fro, no longer trying to conceal its otherworldly qualities.

"But I . . . What are—"

"Feeders, Martin, for those who are so vile that my world is too good for them. And you've let them loose. I warned you, I told you not to open it. All you had to do was your job, but you couldn't. You're fired. Get out."

Martin grabbed his coat off the chair near the computer and ran to the emergency exit at the opposite end of the hallway, up the stairs and out into the bright sun. He stood by his car, wiping puke off his chin, staring wide eyed at the scene around him. Giant maggots with human faces gliding down the nearby residential streets at locomotive speeds. He tried not to think about what he'd seen when grabbing his jacket. The list on the floor near his feet, his name magically being added to the bottom by some invisible hand. He screamed, started the car, and drove to the police station.

Burke was terrified, but he was also angry, and Martin knew he was the focus. The large cop looked down at him and kept shaking his head. Blood ran from his military tattoos, cut when he was thrown to the floor.

"My wife is gone, Martin. They said the whole street was just gone, houses and all, nothing but dirt and scraps of wood. My wife, Martin!"

"I didn't know," Martin said. "How could I know? I just want to go home, play with my dog."

"You have no home anymore, Martin. None of us do. Shit, do you see it out there? It's nothing but death and destruction. Giant worms everywhere you look. Jesus Christ, Martin, I don't know exactly what you did, or how you managed to do it, but you've brought us hell on Earth. You fucked us, Martin, and you killed my wife! You . . . you . . . I'm placing you under arrest."

Martin stood up. "What!"

Burke shoved him against the wall, hard, took out his handcuffs, and latched him to a metal bar in the wall that was installed for just such a purpose. "Shut up, Martin. Here's the thing. People are gonna want someone to blame for this, when and if it goes away. And I'm gonna be the cop who caught the guy that did it. Get me? This kind of thing, people need to know someone paid the price. I need to know you paid the price too. It's human nature, Martin. Trust me, I'm a cop and I know. People need balance, otherwise it's chaos and disorder. It's an eye for an eye."

"But I didn't—"

"Don't matter, Martin. You're gonna help the world get over this soon as we figure out how to stop it. If we can. And the first thing I'm gonna do when the dust settles is get out a press release with your photo on it, give everyone something to look forward to. Then I'm locking you up forever."

"But what about Horris? He's the guy—"

"What Horris! Horris who! We sent ten units to that warehouse! We looked all over, Martin, there's no Horris! There's no computer. No red door. No sign of anyone. It's been abandoned for years. Only thing there was a printout with your name written on it over and over and a lot of weird symbols painted on the walls." Burke went to the window once again, stared out mesmerized the way a child does when he sees Santa Claus at the mall for the first time. "One of these things said your name, Martin, right before it ate a patrolman. Said your name like it was saying grace. It's your fault, Martin. All your fault. You did this to us. Whatever occult bullshit you were playing with. Holy Mary, mother of God . . . "

The building shook, screams filled the air, helicopters and fighter jets rumbled in the distance. A giant shadow lumbered down the city street, blocked out the sun for a minute, and then was gone. Martin cried, thinking about his dog. "I didn't know. I didn't know."

But he knew now where he would eventually end up.

TO PROTECT AND SISSONNE

CHIEF LOGAN MADE his way to the interrogation room and looked through the glass. Inside, officer Johnson, his uniform coated in a mass of blood and gore, danced over to the wall, punched himself in the nose, and spun himself into a leaping split like a world class ballerina.

Officers Burke and Nocks sidled up next to Lawson, waiting for instructions. The rest of the precinct was crowded closely around.

"What the hell was that?" Lawson asked.

Burke pointed at Johnson. "That was a plié, Chief."

"Not the dance. Why's he punching himself in the head?"

"Don't know. The perp was doing the same thing before his head blew up."

"We're sure of that? Johnson didn't shoot him?"

"I checked his weapon when we got him back here. Hasn't been fired."

"How long has he been like this?" Inside the room, Johnson twirled around with his arms splayed out.

"About an hour. Wasn't easy getting him back in the car. Oh, that was a chassé."

Chief Lawson glared at Burke; he was not amused by any of this.

"Sorry," Burke said, "my sister was a dancer, I had to go to all her recitals."

"Tell me about the perp again?"

"Call came in to 911 about 11:30. Guy said he was possessed and couldn't stop dancing. Then he said he'd blow his head off if we didn't bring him an extra large pair of tights."

"This is nuts. If it was somebody's birthday I'd think you were playing a trick on me."

"It's my birthday, chief."

"Shut up, Nocks."

"Shutting up, sir."

Lawson winced as Johnson slammed his fist into his face again before gracefully kicking the air.

"Can we get in there and tie his hands down? He's gonna break his own nose."

"No way," Burke replied. "We already tried. It's like he's got super human strength. He grabbed McCallister and fox-trotted him into the filing cabinet. Knocked him clean out."

"I don't think it was a foxtrot," Nocks said, "looked more like a straight waltz to me."

"No, a waltz goes like this."

Lawson spun around. "Enough! What is this the Pansy Precinct? Jesus Christ. This perp, the one's whose head exploded, was he on any drugs or anything? Maybe Johnson got a dose?"

"Nope," Burke said. "We never got that close. The perp was dancing all over like Fred Astaire. Kept yelling for us to help him. Said his head hurt. Then it just burst. Boom. Brains everywhere. If he'd gotten drugs into Johnson I'd have seen it."

"So then explain . . . this . . . to me." Lawson turned

back and watched Johnson leaping about like a gazelle.

"Don't know. Soon as the guy's head blew off, Johnson says he feels funny. The next thing you know he's moonwalking around.

He was fighting it though, so it was a bad moonwalk. Got him in the car, but by the time I got him here he couldn't withstand it anymore. He's been dancing nonstop since."

"Tell him about the Ouija board." Nocks said to Burke.

"What Ouija board?" Lawson asked

Burke nodded. "The perp had a Ouija board out at his house, like he was playing with contacting spirits."

"Bullshit."

"That's what I said, but when I saw—oh, that was a *poisson*, that's a hard move."

"Burke!"

"Sorry, Chief. The Ouija board. I think the guy was trying to contact a ghost or something. You don't think he's really possessed by a ghost or demon?"

"No such thing as Demons and ghosts, Buffy. This has to be drugs. That would explain the strength. His adrenaline must be through the roof."

"But does adrenaline make your head explode?"

"I've seen drugs do some fucked up shit. Could be."

"I dunno. Some of the things the guy was saying . . . every once in a while he changed voices. This was a big slob of a guy and he knew all about ballet and well, he was pretty graceful, Chief. I don't think a guy that big should have been that graceful. My sister's fat, and she never could do half of what this guy was doing. She's on a diet now though, so I bet if she got back into it—"

"The perp, Burke."

"Right. I don't think drugs make you dance like that. I mean, this guy could have been on *So You Think You Can Dance* or something . . . 'cept for the part where his head exploded."

"So the guy was a good dancer. Doesn't mean anything."

"Well, like I said, he was speaking in two voices. One was a regular guy like you'd expect, and the other was a French accent. I think. And then when Johnson was in the car he started speaking in a French accent, too. Johnson speaks a little Spanish but no French. My sister took French growing up and—"

"Mention your sister again and I'm shooting you in the face."

"Point is, Chief, I think he's really possessed."

"Burke, you'll never make detective if you don't get your head out of your ass." Lawson went over to the door to the interrogation room and grabbed the handle. "Okay, I'm gonna go in and try to subdue him. Nocks, you come with me. Burke, you stay here in case he gets by us. You, over there, go get a doctor."

"But I don't work here," responded the delivery boy from Smitty's Sandwich Shop.

"You're here now so do it before I arrest you."

"You think a doctor can fix this?" Burke asked.

"If he's on drugs I want his system pumped."

Lawson opened the door and stepped into the room. His uniform slick with the perp's brains, Jonhson saw the Chief and danced over to him, smiled and kept spinning. "Johnson, stop moving."

Johnson spun away, punched himself

in the face again. "Oh God, Chief. I can't! My head hurts so bad! It feels like—"

And suddenly Johnson's voice slid into a high pitched nasally accent. "Bon jour, Messieur. Come to challenge me for a position in the Royal Dance Company? I dare say you are out of your league. Can you do this?"

Johnson leapt though the air and made himself straight as an arrow. From outside the room, Lawson heard Burke remark about the quality of the move.

"Johnson, I need you to stop moving. Can you do that?"

Johnson's voice came back as he twirled on one leg. "Chief. I can't control anything. I can't— You're friend is mine, Mr. Gendarme. But no worries, I am almost done with him. So quickly the body tires. And this one has been a fighter."

Seeing this was going nowhere, Lawson signaled for Nocks to move around the back of the dancing officer. Cautiously, Nocks followed the instructions, fear visibly wrinkled into his face.

"Nocks, when I say go, we grab him. Ready...go!"

Together, Lawson and Nocks lunged for Officer Johnson, but the cop gracefully spun and kicked Nocks in the head, sending him to the floor. Without stopping the spin, the officer then grabbed

Lawson and pulled him close like a dance partner. Lawson fought to pull free of the grip but the cop was too strong. They danced around the perimeter of the room like two highschoolers at a sock hop.

"You cannot stop the dance, Mr. Gendarme," Johnson said in the French accent again. "It is forever in our lives, like the spinning of the earth itself. But alas, this body is exhausted, and so I bid you a brief adieu."

Without warning, Johnson stopped dancing, his eyes slowly focusing on the crowd watching him. Was he back to normal? Lawson wondered.

"Johnson? You okay? You just kicked Nocks in the face. I called for a doctor so just sit down for a second and—"

Johnson threw his arms to

his head and screamed. "Oh God, Chief! My head! My—"

There was a loud pop and Lawson froze as Johnson's head exploded all over him.

The other officers rushed in to the room, some with their guns drawn.

Lawson, his face dripping with bits of Johnson's skull, shouted to his men. "Put your guns down, you idiots! I didn't shoot him! Burke, where's the doctor?"

"On his way, Chief."

"Jesus! Someone get a HAZMAT team out to the perp's house! This has got to be a bio-weapon. I want...all units...all units...I feel kind of . . . "

Burke put a hand on his boss' shoulder, winced

when he realized he was touching his former partner's brains. "Chief, are you all right?

"Get off me. I'm fine. I . . . I . . . kind of feel like dancing, actually."

"Chief?"

"My head feels woozy. I . . . I . . . "

Lawson could feel the urge to spin welling up inside him, a power that bordered on the insatiable. Oh God, it was killing him, he needed to move, to leap and twirl. In his mind's eye he saw a thin man dressed in a black leotard, waving at him, laughing. The man grew larger and larger.

He wanted to shout at the man but found his voice was not his own. He spoke aloud to the room. "I am the greatest dancer to ever grace the stages of Paris. Do not fight me you stinky gendarmes, or I will clout this man's jaw as such."

Lawson punched himself in the nose.

The officers backed off.

With a graceful arch, Lawson said, "And now, we dance." He broke into a sissonne and it felt oh so good.

BROTHERS TILL THE END

THERE WAS A knock at the window. Mathew rolled over and opened his eyes, saw four men with machetes and jack-o-lanterns for heads standing against the wall. Wait, that couldn't be right. people didn't have pumpkin heads. The nightmare he'd been dragged from was mixing with reality, like thick creamer in coffee.

He shook his head and the men disappeared in a smoky wisp. He looked at the clock, saw that it was 3:42 in the morning, cursed, and closed his eyes again.

The knock came again, louder this time. Mathew shot upright in bed, reached for his bedside lamp and flipped the switch but the light didn't come on. He stared into the darkness.

Did he really hear a knock? He was sure the noise had been real.

He watched the window for a minute. Nothing happened. His eyes grew heavy. He cursed again, laid his head back on his pillow.

Again, a loud rap on the window, a bang, and a voice, "Matty, let me in, it's freezing out here."

His eyes jolted open. Okay, he thought, that I heard.

"Matty, Jesus Christ already."

A chill raced down his spine. No, it couldn't be, he thought. He knew that voice, knew it so well to know it couldn't be who it sounded like. His older brother Gordon had been dead for over four months now. Killed in a hunting accident. Mathew had made his peace with it. They all had. It wasn't Gordon, it couldn't be.

"Some welcome home party this is," the voice said. "Matty, if you don't open the window I'm gonna break it down."

Flinging back the covers, Mathew moved cautiously over to the window. Through the sheer curtain, he could see the night sky was abnormally dark.

The silhouette of a dark, human moved on the other side. The shape and build were similar to Gordon. The figure raised its arm and hit the pane again with a jerky, uncontrolled swing, as if its arm was asleep.

Bang!

Mathew's eyes went wide. I'm two stories up, he thought. Who the hell is standing on a ladder outside my bedroom window on a Wednesday night—correction: Thursday morning—imitating my dead brother?

Snatching up his baseball bat from where it slept on the floor near a collection of comic books, Mathew walked slowly to the window and slid the curtain aside. "What the . . . !"

Dropping the bat, he quickly backpedaled across the dark bedroom, stepping over video games and dirty clothes, until he hit the wall and could go no further. He stared in horror at what he saw.

On the other side of the window, worms digging in and out of its flesh, was his dead, rotting brother Gordon.

"Hi, Matty," it said.

How else to think of it, Mathew thought, but as an *it*. Flesh was peeling off its face, bone peeking out from where the skin had decayed; a clump of hair fell out and fluttered to the ground two stories below. The black suit it had been buried in was still in good shape, albeit covered in dirt and weeds and a few wriggling maggots.

"You gonna let me in or what, dicknose?"

"No. No, this isn't real, I'm dreaming."

"Wrongo, compadre. I'm real and I need to talk to you. It's important."

"Go away. You're not real." Mathew began pinching himself, hitting his head against the wall. "Wake up, Matt, wake up."

"You're gonna give yourself a goose egg on your head. And you'll wake up Mom and Dad and I can't afford to have them see me like this."

"What do you want?"

"What, do you have wax in your ears? I want to come in. I'm freezing my ass off."

Mathew shook his head, felt his way along the wall until he got to the light switch. He flipped it up but, like the bedside lamp, nothing happened.

"Had to mess with the lighting, bro. Sorry, but bright light hurts my eyes."

Quickly, Mathew ran and picked up the bat from where he'd dropped it, held it like he was Hank Aaron. Through the window, he could see Gordon's body drifting sideways as if on a wire.

It's floating in the air, he realized.

"How do I know you're Gordon. Give me some sign."

The thing that used to be Gordon held up its middle finger. "Let me in or I'll hold you down and slap you like I did in front of Julie Marston. She made fun of you for weeks."

Yeah, she did, thought Mathew. It really is Gordon.

Relaxing his grip, he moved to the window and unlatched it. Still holding the bat, he lifted the window and stepped back. Like a feather in the breeze, the rotted corpse drifted into the room and sat on the bed.

"Thanks, bro," it said, "didn't know how much longer I could stay out there. The cold affects my movements."

"I can't believe—"

"Yeah, well, believe it. I have something to tell you."

As it spoke a chunk of flesh slid off its neck and fell to its lap.

Where the flesh had been, a gaping hole now revealed a blackened trachea.

"Look at me, I'm falling apart at the fucking seams."

"How can you be alive?"

"Interesting little fact . . . the dead, it turns out, get one opportunity to return here. Sort of like a phone call from jail. Can use it whenever you want. Most people don't know what to use it for, and some end up never using it. One guy I met—he got eaten by a tiger shark—he wants to visit the first alien leader that enslaves the human race. Funny guy. Anyway where was I?"

"Something you needed to tell me."

"Oh yeah. Something is going to happen to you.

You're going to be hit by a truck."

"What!"

"Relax, I can change it. That's why I'm here." The corpse stood up from the bed and glided over to the closet, floating over all the dirty clothes. It had amazingly good eyesight considering how dark it was in the room. It reached up to the shelf where Mathew kept some boxes of baseball cards, a few old toys, and three porno magazines hidden under sweatshirts. It lifted the sweatshirts and looked at the magazines.

"Just making sure it's girls. Never really knew with you."

"Boy, even in death you can still be a prick."

"Get over it." The corpse held up its hand, pushed on the ceiling until its hand went through the plaster When it pulled its hand back it was holding a tiny tin box. It floated over to Mathew and handed it to him.

Taking it from his dead brother, Mathew turned it over and studied it. He'd never seen the box before, had no idea how it had gotten up in the ceiling. It was old, perhaps from the '30s, with pictures of cigars on it. A vintage cigar box, he realized. He'd seen them drawn in comics but had never seen a real one until now.

"Go ahead, dipshit, open it."

Finally putting the bat down, Mathew opened the top of the box. Inside was a folded piece of paper, yellowed from age. Taking it out, he could feel the brittleness of it, as if it would fall apart at the slightest breeze. He unfolded it carefully. There were words on it, written in a script he could barely make out.

"An old woman, Grace Millington, gave me this when I was seventeen," Gordon's corpse said. "She was the Madame of a whore house upstate I used to go to. Also dabbled in the occult. Weird, I know. But...best pussy in town, and they didn't check IDs. Man, those girls taught me a thing or two. I'd give you the address but they tore it down few years ago. Well read the damn thing already."

Mathew read the note: "Eternal life for the lifeless. Food for the hungry. Soil removed, blood infused, the walkers may return."

Gordon's corpse chuckled, decaying skin and dust puffing out of its mouth. "God, it sounds so stupid."

Mathew looked up at his dead brother, felt a cold breeze blow in the window from outside. The moon had emerged from behind the clouds, though the night sky seemed blacker now than before. "What does it mean?"

"It means you get a second chance. All you have to do is say it. Which, I guess you just did. So...that truck should miss you now."

"A truck kills me?"

"Tomorrow, on your way to school. But now . . . I figured, how cruel to die before you get your dick wet."

"Hey, I'm not a virgin."

"And I'm not dead. Jerking off doesn't count, But-twipe."

"You came back to save me so I could have sex."

"Jesus, you're dense. The sex was a joke. I came back to give you a second chance at life. Make it count okay."

"Wait . . . this paper . . . . This Madame knew I was going to die?"

"No, she knew *I* was going to die. The note was for me but I never read it. Dad put it in the attic with a bunch of my stuff when I left for college. Listen, I have to go, my head is barely hanging on by a tendon as it is." The corpse stood up and started gliding to the window. Mathew reached out and grabbed its shoulder.

"Wait!"

Gordon's arm snapped off in Mathew's hand, like a dry branch breaking off a tree. Screaming, Mathew dropped it and fell backwards and tired to regain his composure.

Still gliding, Gordon's corpse bent down and picked it up. "Fuck, now look what you did. What the hell am I supposed to do with only one arm? Guess I could use it as a weapon or something."

Rising slowly, Mathew wiped the sweat off his brow. "Sorry. I just . . . I wanted to ask . . . "

"What it's like? What it feels like to be dead?"

Mathew nodded eagerly. Gordon's corpse threw the arm over its shoulder like it was a mink stole. A piece of bone fell out of the hole in its shoulder. "It ain't so bad, really. You get updates on your friends and family. And mostly you just hang out in big malls with others. All that shit they say about dead celebrities playing poker together is true. I tried to play with John Belushi but he told me fuck off. Sometimes I'm not so sure it's even heaven. I mean, there's no real indication of what it is. Just lots of malls and coffee shops and sometimes there's screaming and sometimes there's laughter. Haven't found any whorehouses yet. Mostly, it's just boring. A lot like being alive."

With that, the rotted body headed back toward the window once again. Despite the creepiness of the whole affair, Mathew felt overwhelmed with emotion. What do I say, he thought, that conveys my gratitude. My dead brother just came back from the grave to save my life. I have to tell him something. Problem was, Mathew had never really liked his brother all that much. Gordon had been such a prick to him all the time. Beating him up in front of girls, switching his school lunches with bags of dog shit. Then there was the time he put the poison ivy under his pillow. Mathew's face had blown up so bad he needed to go get a shot at the hospital.

As the corpse began to float through the window once more, Mathew felt that, perhaps, those were the things older brothers did. In time, they would have matured and become good friends, like in the movies. He did come back to save me, he reminded himself.

"Hey, Gordon . . . "

Halfway out the window, Gordon turned around. "Yeah?"

"Thanks. I wish you could have lived so we could have become friends. But I'm glad to know you're not such a bad guy after all."

The rotting Gordon looked out at the moon, down at the ground outside, back at Mathew. There was a gurgling crunching sound audible in the air outside the house. Mathew cocked his head, suddenly aware of the noise.

A smile stretched across Gordon's decomposing face. He spoke, but not to Mathew. He spoke to somebody outside. "Jesus H. Christ on a flaming surfboard, took you guys long enough."

From outside there was a grunt, followed by a long moan. Two hands appeared on the window sill beside Gordon's corpse. They hauled up a face. A rotting face, tongue lolling to the side, eyes dazed.

Mathew's jaw fell open "What the . . . ?"

"Boy, you always were a dummy, Matty. I told them you were easy prey."

The new corpse slid inside Mathew's room, groaned as it smelled flesh. Behind it, another dead body was being helped in by Gordon. "Come and get it while it's hot, boys," Gordon laughed.

"What're you doing, Gordy!" Mathew was wide-eyed, making for the door.

"We're hungry, Matty," Gordy's corpse said. "We need food. Don't take it personally. I just never liked you is all."

"But the letter . . . I thought you came to save me?"

"You would believe that. That letter is meaningless, it was part of a song I wrote when I was in a band in high school, The Skullfuckers. God we sucked."

"But . . . but . . . everything you said."

"I was just biding time till my friends got here. See, we're coming back to take over the land. I figure I'll give

Dad and Mom a fighting chance, but you....nah. Now, it's dinner time."

"No!" Quickly, Mathew snatched up the bat, swung it at the first corpse. Its head ripped off and smashed against the wall. But it was too little too late. The room was now full of the dead, reaching and drooling for his flesh. They floated in through the window like giant, bloody dust motes. Hands grabbed his hair, pulled him to the floor. He felt teeth sink into this flesh.

"You're such an asshole, Gordy!"

Through bulging eyes, Mathew watched as the rotted, black teeth pulled his raw flesh from is bones. The pain was agonizing! He screamed in and fought but they tore chunks of him away like he'd fallen under a farm tractor. The more he struggled the easier his flesh tore loose.

He managed to get out one last scream before his mouth was ripped off: "You...asshole!"

The last thing he heard before the blackness took him was Gordon's reply. "That's what big brothers are for, dipshit."

THE HALLOWED SHORTCUT

MS. GULLIVAN'S HOUSE. What a target! Every Halloween she gave us the worst candy, and every Halloween we paid her back somehow.

From the street, Derek urged me on. "Mike, c'mon, before the second coming."

I turned to him, again admiring his X-Wing Pilot costume, and gave him a thumbs-up. Then I put my foot through Ms. Gullivan's jack-o-lantern with as much force as I could find in me. *Splootch!* Pumpkin exploded into the air, covering the steps, the door, and my hooker costume. My leg got tangled in the damn dress and I almost took a digger into the bushes that lined her house.

"Hell yeah!" Derek shouted. "F Ms. Gullivan in the A! Ugly old bitch."

I rushed back toward the street, trying to shake pumpkin out of my dress; I was already coated in it from the previous house's pumpkin, which had been painted like a vampire until I'd put my foot through it. Together, Derek and I had destroyed just about every jack-o-lantern in the neighborhood, as was our annual MO on this night.

"This shit is getting sticky," I said, walking beside him down Pepper Drive, noticing how his once white Rebel Alliance helmet was splotched with orange goo. It was nearing ten o'clock and most trick-or-treaters were done for the night. Porch lights were extinguishing around us as the neighborhood went to bed. Only the squealing of tires on a nearby street spoke of any teenage hooligans still up to no good. Aside from us, anyway.

Overhead, the tawny moon was emerging from behind a patch of clouds like a fish eye rolling out to peek at us. All the pumpkin pulp on me was starting to stink. It wasn't so much the wetness that bugged me as the consistency of it. Try as I might to pull it from my costume, I only succeeded in gluing my fingers together.

"Nasty," I said, whipping some at Derek. "That was a good one, huh?"

"That thing erupted," he replied. "Yo, you got some in your eyebrows."

I ran my arm across my head and it came away orange. That was enough to make me feel a little queasy. I didn't even like pumpkin pie; this was starting to wig me out.

A muzak version of Green Day's "American Idiot" interrupted our chit-chat. Derek pulled out his cell phone and flipped it open, scowled. "Sonofa . . . my mom's texting me. She wants me home. She's on some new pill and it blows her anxiety through the roof."

"She should take something for that."

"She does, another pill, but it gives her gas so only she only takes it when she sleeps. If she's awake she's on my case like a dog on a chick's panties."

"That's cool. I wanna go home and shower anyway. This pumpkin reeks. I smell like this Monday in homeroom and Danielle ain't gonna say two words to me."

"And that's different from any other day how?"

"Man, shut up. You don't know. She talked to me yesterday."

"You mean when she told you to stop kicking her chair?"

"Whatever," I replied, unhappy with this line of conversation. "You wanna cut across the park?"

"Nah, I heard Hutcher and his gang were rolling a keg out there tonight, getting loaded and jumping kids. He's crazy —Hannibal Lector crazy. Let's just cut through that field behind the mortuary. It comes out a street over from my house."

I nodded. We were no strangers to the shortcut. Only reason we didn't take it more often was because a) it was full of thorn bushes, and b) well you know, too many horror movies. But I'd take real life zombies over Hutcher and his primate army of thugs any day.

Throwing our candy-filled pillowcases over our shoulders, we turned onto Howell Street, hoofed it down Union, and took a left on Bishop Drive, which was one of those streets with businesses at one end and homes at the other. The mortuary was the last business before the homes started, flanked on the other side by a card shop. Behind it was a large field that used to have a swing set for the owners' kids. But the kids were in college now and the swing set had been replaced by more thorn bushes. Beyond the field, though, was a thicket of trees through which a small creek ran. And finally, after that, was Derek's street. I lived a few blocks away from him.

We made a couple of jokes about ghosts as we started across the field. My dress immediately got caught on the thorns—it's not like I knew enough to hike it up or anything—and Derek swore up a storm trying a new, and ultimately idiotic, approach that involved running through them at full speed.

Not a good idea, I assure you.

In the sky above, clouds completely swallowed the moon back into oblivion. And by the time we reached the creek it was so dark I had to use peripheral vision to see where I was going.

"Okay, that was a shit idea," Derek said, showing me his bloody palms. "Note to self, thorn bushes suck ass."

"Suck it up, Jedi."

As the crickets chirped, we tread slowly into the black treeline, holding our hands out to avoid running into branches. The stench of the creek greeted us before we even saw it— a combination of mud and algae, probably some dead rodents decomposing, far overpowering the sweeter aromas of autumnal leaves on the ground. Taking deep breaths, we leapt across the creek — which was about five feet wide —landing on flat, dry ground on the other side. From there it was up a small incline (and through more thicket) to the backyard of the Felton house.

Missy Felton was a year younger than us, a sophomore now, and but was more popular than we could ever hope to be. And the way I felt about Danielle, that's how Derek felt about Missy Felton.

"Shit," Derek said, reaching the chain link fence that lined the Felton property, "that's Missy right there, on the back porch. What's she doing?"

"Looks like she's on the phone."

Derek ducked down. "Dammit, I can't go through there."

"Dude, she won't know it's you. Unless she has the Force or something. What's her midichlorian count?"

"Man, F that midichlorian crap in the A. That crap is so lame."

"You're a tool. C'mon, let's just run."

"No way, man, I don't want her to see me like this."

"Then why'd you dress like that?"

"Because *Star Wars* kicks your ass."

"I thought you said—"

"Original trilogy, Jackoff. Look, I ain't stupid, she'll call me a geek. I'm not going through there."

"Then what?"

Grabbing my shoulder strap, Derek led me north along the backs of the properties. All of them were fenced off, and a few of them had mongrels sleeping in doghouses that woke at our twig-snapping footsteps. One had a motion sensor that lit up the trees like a spotlight, so we jogged faster, leaving a trail of barking dogs in our wake.

"Here," Derek said, hopping over a small picket fence into someone's backyard.

I followed suit, landing in a large garden, right near a little flagstone path that cut through the center of it. From what we could see by the half-moon, the house was dark and rundown. Plywood covered the upstairs windows. The back porch was overrun with dying plants, snaking weeds, and cobwebs. The paint was peeling off and the shutters where hanging lopsided like they'd given up on life. The whole structure was aged and brittle. We were off track, behind a different street now, and I couldn't place what house it was. As we moved farther into the yard, the moon found a break in the clouds and stared down at us, bathing the garden in a golden hue. And our eyes went wide.

All around us—pumpkins. I mean a shit-load of pumpkins. I could barely see any grass at all. Just pumpkins pumpkins pumpkins. Everywhere.

"That's a big ass pumpkin patch," I said.

"Yeah. Jesus, it's the mother-load."

"Who grows a pumpkin patch like this in their yard? Who lives here?" I stepped a couple feet into the patch and nudged a pumpkin with my shoe.

"Fucked if I know. But they need to call Bob Villa, this place looks like ass."

"Look at 'em all."

"Mike, you thinking what I'm thinking?"

No answer was needed. I drew my foot back and made like a soccer star. There was a wet thud as pulp shot out toward Derek, hitting his jumpsuit. With a spirited curse, he picked up the nearest pumpkin and hurled it at my feet. It shattered and sent seeds and gook into my face.

And the fight was on.

Pumpkins, pulp, seeds, stems, all of it smashing and

exploding and covering us in thick gobs. Our silent laughing had us doubled over with good pain, sticky pumpkin raining down everywhere. Within minutes we were drenched in slime. We laughed as quietly as we could until we thought we might pass out, then caught our breath and stood looking at the mess.

"I win!" I declared.

"No way, I nailed you in the face with that last one."

"My face? You should look in a mirror, Luke Sky-farter. I could stick your head in an oven and make a pie."

"C'mon, Jar Jar," Derek said, all the pumpkins now smashed, "my mom's gonna have my ass." He picked up his pillowcase full of candy and made his way up the path toward the back of the house, pulling seeds from his collar. Shadows drifted over the yard as the moon decided there was nothing more to see. The clouds were twice as thick, the darkness twice as black. The scent of pumpkin hung in the air and once again made me a little queasy.

I noticed a small pumpkin near my foot that had survived. Aha, I thought, here was a chance for one more hurrah. I picked it up and aimed for Derek. In the darkness, he was a mere ink spot. I wound up, concentrated, made sure my grip was good . . .

. . . and a large black shape came out of nowhere and stood in front of me.

As human as it was, it was something more. Its legs, torso, and arms were reedy and thin. It was taller than us by a good foot. But the head—the head was huge. I mean way out of proportion. At first I thought it was a costume, maybe a space helmet, but there was something odd about it. It wasn't round enough, more, well, ovoid and misshapen. A strange cowlick stuck up on top.

"Nooo!" it bellowed.

I froze. The small pumpkin, somehow of its own accord, rolled from my hand and split on some flag- stone.

"My flock," the shadowy figure growled. The voice was low, gurgling, like someone talking through a mouthful of soup. "What have you done? My little ba- bies." The figure lunged at Derek, grabbed him by the shoulder.

"Look, mister," Derek yelled, his Rebel Alliance helmet momentarily down over his eyes as the shape shook him, "it wasn't us, we just got here."

Stupid lie, I thought. Wouldn't take a detective to know we were the ones who busted up the pumpkins. I mean, we were covered in it. Better come clean I fig- ured, lust apologize and be on our way. But I never got chance. The figure roared, a guttural resonance. Un- natural. Otherworldly. Derek shrieked. My knees buck- led like a rickety step ladder. The large shape hurled my friend across the yard like he was a rag doll. I stood in horror as Derek came to rest near the back porch of the house.

Couldn't really see him through the darkness, but I could tell he wasn't moving. He'd hit hard and gone limp. Then the figure fumed and, though I couldn't make out its features, I knew it was staring at me.

When it came toward me, it walked like a stick bug, skinny legs extending outward and bending nearly in half. Its gait was slow but its stride was long. And I thought, Jesus Christ, it's not human!

The closer it got, the more I couldn't move. "You will pay for this," it gurgled. "Pay dearly."

Large round head, stick-like body, it covered the space between us in seconds. Finding my feet, I dropped my bag of candy and tore back over the fence, into the woods, moving on sheer adrenaline. Behind me I could hear it closing in, could hear branches breaking and twigs snapping as it crashed through anything in its way, could hear the wet voice repeating, "my flock," over and over.

The woods were beyond black, the kind of darkness where you can literally put your hand in front of your face and not see it. Trees came out of nowhere and pounded me, stabbed my legs and raked my face. A sickness filled my gut, but I kept running, praying and hoping I didn't trip and fall. Branches broke behind me like automatic gunfire as the thing chasing me blazed straight through whatever was in its path.

And then I was tumbling. A root caught my foot, spun me around, throwing me to the ground so hard my teeth almost came out the back of my skull. As I landed on damp earth, the creature came out of the darkness and stood above me, a black silhouette. The head, huge and engulfed in the shadows of the woods, bent down toward me. I smelled pumpkin – on me, in the air, everywhere.

Crab-walking backward, I heard myself say, "Please, please leave me alone. I didn't mean to..."

The large creature followed, lording over me. "You are beyond forgiveness. You murdered them."

"I don't' understand—"

"WHY!" The trees rumbled at its voice, as if they were playing jury to its judge. "WHY!"

"Please . . . " My hands went up over my eyes, like I was a little kid again. Like, if I could not see it, it wouldn't hurt me. And just like a scared kid, I peeked out between my fingers as the large head swam right up against mine. Whether my eyes had adjusted to the dark, or if some faint illumination burned out of its triangular eyes, I couldn't be sure. Whether the zigzag mouth was real or a trick of the shadows in the trees, I couldn't tell. Whether the sallow skin tone was real or a trick of the emerging moon, I couldn't tell. All I knew for sure was that my crotch became hot and wet, and a dog was barking a few feet away on the other side of a nearby fence.

"Dammit, dog, shut up!"

Who was that? The dog's owner? Maybe a neighbor trying to sleep? I didn't know. And I didn't care. Whoever it was, they were my saving grace. The thing trying to peer through my fingers stood up, looked toward the dog, and crashed back through the woods the way it had come. Blood rushed to my head and before I could scream for help I got dizzy and closed my eyes. I felt myself swimming.

• • •

WHEN I OPENED my eyes, it was still dark and damn cold out. My dress clung to me, the pumpkin and urine, dried and crusty, smelled so caustic I dry-heaved for a second. Climbing over another fence into the closest yard was damn near impossible because I couldn't stop my legs from shaking. There was a doghouse there but the dog was gone. Maybe the owner had brought it in for the night.

I ran around the house, onto the street where I got my bearings, and then several blocks over to my own house. On the door, a note from my mom scolded me for coming home late and told me to lock up. I fumbled my key out of my pocket and tried to steady myself enough to unlock the door. Just when I opened it, a hand landed on my shoulder.

"Ah!"

Spinning around, I found Derek behind me. He was covered in dirt, like he'd been slinking through bushes. A gash ran across his forehead.

"Hurry up!" he said. "Hurry up! It's looking for me."

No, it couldn't be. But Derek's saucer eyes said it was true.

We threw ourselves inside and ran down the hall to my room. The house was dark, the refrigerator humming in the kitchen. The clock in my bedroom said 1:24.

"Don't turn the light on," Derek said. "I don" think

it knows we're here. The last thing you want is for it to know where you live."

A moment of silence passed between us.

"Where the hell were you?' Derek finally asked. "I've been hiding in bushes forever. What the hell is that thing?"

"Don't know. I can't believe you got away."

"No thanks to you."

"How?"

"I hit my head when it threw me, but I woke up a minute later and booked outta there. You left me, asshole."

He must have escaped when the thing was chasing me.

"We gotta call the police," he said.

"And say what?"

"Say anything. Say you've got a bomb. I don't care, just call them."

"I'm waking up my parents."

Just then there was a tap on my bedroom window. We froze. Our breaths escaped us. Turning slowly, we looked at the window. My house was one story, my bedroom window on the front side looking out toward the street. Only blue curtains separated us from whatever was outside tapping on the window. But the silhouette...the silhouette was plain as day. Large round head, stick-like arm tapping methodically. *Tap tap.*

Derek put his finger to his mouth, shushing me. As if I could find my voice anyway.

The figure stood still for a moment, then disappeared from the window. We listened as it made its way around to the other side of the house, its footsteps crunching the dead grass in the yard. Opening my bedroom door, we stepped into the hallway. The footsteps sounded near the kitchen windows now. Together, we stepped lightly toward the humming refrigerator, stood there listening.

That's when it passed in front of the window over the sink, the large orange head turning to look in. Its triangle eyes burned bright yellow, its black, crooked mouth tight with hatred. It was a brief glimpse, but long enough for our hearts to lurch out of our chests.

Continuing past the kitchen, it stopped near the family room, tapped on the window. *Tap tap.* We stood still, crouched down in the shadows near the refrigerator. I realized I was crying. I also realized that Derek's phone was playing *American Idiot.*

"Turn it off! Hurry!" I whispered.

He fumbled it out of his pocket and tore the battery out. "Please leave," he prayed. "Please leave."

But it didn't leave. It came back, back to the kitchen window, its bulbous orange head leaning forward to spy through the glass. There was no way we could move without it seeing us—we were trapped next to the refrigerator. Had it heard the phone? It must have. Derek was crying now too.

The round head pressed in closer, touching the glass now. From its black triangular nose, it huffed condensation onto the window pane. Long reedy fingers came up and wiped away a circle in the condensation. The fingers scratched on the pane like sticks. Tilting its head, it looked in and scanned my kitchen, blinked a couple of times, and then tapped on the glass.

Why was it tapping? To let us know it found us? To draw us out? Jesus, it wouldn't leave. It knew where we were. As a testament to that fact, its reedy fingers worked their way under the frame of the window and gave it a little yank. The latch was on, though, so the window wouldn't rise, it just rattled a bit.

Looking in once again, scanning the kitchen, it ran its fingers around the outer edge of the window, tapping it every so often. *Tap tap.* Trying to get in, I realized. Looking for a way to open the window.

Derek said, "Just go away." And the large head, fast as lightning, pasted its triangular eyes to the window pane and locked on Derek's voice . . . looking toward the shadows near the refrigerator . . . toward us, knowing exactly where we were.

It's going to get and kill us, I thought.

Then, from the street, there came a familiar voice. "Let's go to my house, my old man has beer in the fridge." It was Hutcher and his gang. I never felt so happy to hear his voice. They whooped and laughed and made the usual obnoxious noise they always made walking through the neighborhood. The large orange head snapped back from the window, not wanting to risk exposure. Faintly, we heard it walk around to the front yard, cross the street and disappear. It was gone.

● ● ●

THE NEXT MORNING was full of activity. Both Derek and I told our parents what happened. The police accompanied us and our dads to the dilapidated house to confirm the assault. "This where the pumpkins are?" one of the cops asked me.

"Yeah, right here," Derek said. We all walked around to the backyard. The pumpkins were gone. I mean all of them. Not a trace remained.

"What the . . . " I stuttered.

The cops went into the abandoned house and came out a few minutes later. "Nothing in there. Just cobwebs and faded wallpaper."

"I'm telling you," I said, "there was a pumpkin patch right here. Maybe a hundred of them. And that thing came out of the house."

My dad was giving me the evil eye. Fibbing did not go over well in my household. Derek's dad wasn't much happier.

Finally, one of the cops spoke. "Well, busy night last night. It was probably that Hutcher kid. That one's headed for juvie, trust me. Look, I'll go over and talk to him, tell him to leave you alone. You two just stay out of his way if you can."

Derek and I just nodded. They weren't going to believe us. It was pointless to argue. The creature had gone, moved to a new lair. It must have known we'd come back with other people. Thing like that, it hadn't survived on just luck, it knew how to hide.

We walked home, our dads talking to each other about football. I can't remember what Derek and I talked about. I just kept thinking that it knew where I lived. And I wondered how long it would be before I heard the tapping again.

GINSU GARY

"SO, LIKE, WHAT . . . you're just gonna take the body somewhere and bury it?"

Ginsu Gary stares back at the small effete man standing in the corner. The man wears a tan suite pollocked with the deceased's brains. His shoulders are hunched, head hanging low, like he's trying to compact himself. Like a little boy acting coy, he scuffs his feet against the hardwood floor, then takes out a cigarette and lights it up. "Stupid fucker gave me a hard time," the man says. "I was hoping he'd take his lumps like a man. Guess they never do, huh?"

Ginsu Gary surveys the scene. One dead double-crossing thief and former employee of the Bernardo Family sits tied to a chair, fingers smashed by a hammer, eyes black from a broken nose, one well-placed bullet in his head.

"I don't bury, sir," says Ginsu Gary, "I clean. Is this his house? It's dirty."

The smoking man looks around the dilapidated living room. There is nothing much to speak of beyond a couch, a TV, and a throw rug that might have once been completely white but now looks like cow hide thanks to a dozen brown stains.

"Of course, it's his house. You think I'd do it at my place? Boss said to get this done ASAP. I didn't have time to drag him to the woods or nothing. Shitty place, huh? Guy's wife left him years ago, guess she took the home furnishings with her too. Bitches will do that. Think they own everything. What are you doing?"

Ginsu Gary sets a black alligator skin suitcase down on the floor, opens it up and reaches inside. From within he removes a large steel knife that catches the light of the wan overhead bulb. He removes a clear plastic sheath from the blade, tosses that back in the suitcase. The knife is big, would probably do well in a sword fight. The bare steel catches the light again and throws stars onto the walls. He removes a black shammy from the suitcase, cleans the blade for good measure, stuffs it in his pocket, and approaches the dead man.

"You know what this guy did?" asks Smoking Man. "I'll tell you what he did. Boss has him deliver those packages to the Minnie Mouse Crew down in National City, you know. He brings the stuff, they push it, gets himself a courier's cut and all that. For every twenty packages he gets down there, Boss lets him play the tables at the Mai Tai Room . . . on the house. Thing is, ol' Georgie here had himself a real gambling problem. Only Boss doesn't know that. He just thinks he's being a generous employer letting Georgie into the back rooms where the big money is on the table. But that's not my point—whoa! You gonna do that right here?"

Ginsu Gary places the butcher's knife against Georgie's throat and begins making mental assessments about where to make his cuts. "Yes. Don't worry, sir, this will just take a moment. Do you have a moment, sir?"

"Yeah. You want a tarp or something? That's gonna be messy."

"Do I look like I'd leave a mess here?" Ginsu Gary smiles wide, exposing snow white teeth that are perfectly symmetrical. "No, sir, I won't. But it's okay, I understand your worry. 'Who's this guy,' you're asking. 'Who's this guy acting like he knows stuff.' I get that a lot." He chuckles and dips his head in a friendly acknowledging manner. "No, sir, you are in good hands. This is why I'm here. You were saying?"

"Yeah right. So Georgie develops himself a nice little gambling problem, and decides he's gonna lift every tenth package or so. I mean, he's the only liaison to the Minnies so how's the boss gonna find out if he don't tell on himself. But Boss ain't stupid, you know. Hell I was just gonna tell him to take the money back, but the fucker goes and gets pushy with me. Dumb motherfucker. So I call Boss and he says just do the guy already, that's he's done with him anyway."

Ginsu Gary places one hand on dead Georgie's head, and tilts it back to better expose the neck. With a gentle, almost graceful move, he places the knife once again against Georgie's neck. "Do you have knives in your home, Mr. . . . "

"Hey oh. No names."

"What can I call you then?" Ginsu Gary glances sideways, waiting for an answer.

Smoking Man considers his options. "How about Mr. Kent. Kind of a Superman fan."

"Well who isn't. Let me ask you again, Mr. Kent, do

you have knives in your home?"

"Yeah, sure, why?"

"What would you say if I told you this knife could cut through bone and still stay sharp enough to carve a roast right after."

This makes Mr. Kent laugh, pull on his cigarette, which smokes in blue hues. Somewhere outside in the night, a siren dopplers by without further thought. Kent looks to the window and studies the closed blinds, then returns his smile to Ginsu Gary. "I'd say you've got yourself a good knife, I guess."

"It's not just a good knife, Mr. Kent, it's a Carving Cobra C-100. Let me show you how well it works. Can I do that for you?"

"Hey, man, please do. I gotta get this taken care of and get back to the Boss's place to figure out how we're gonna deal with the Minnies now, who waited this fucking long to tell us they were getting stiffed. You'd think those slit-eyed Tokyo drifting motherfuckers woulda spoken up sooner. Yakuza my ass. They know shit about business. Course they ain't Yakuza for real, but you get my vibe."

"If you'll notice, the C-100 Carving Cobra is made of one hundred percent American stainless steel. See how easy it slices through the bone." Ginsu Gary draws the blade across Georgie's neck and a torrent of blood spurts forth like ejaculate. Somehow, it misses getting on Ginsu Gary's blue button down shirt. "You'd think the bone would be a problem, Mr. Kent, but not for the Carving Cobra C-100. See how it slips right through the vertebrae in just one . . . two . . . ”

Mr. Kent turns away, disgusted and nearly drops his cigarette. "Oh man, that's gross. Sheesh, I thought you was joking. Thought you was gonna bag him up and move him first. Oh fuck. I'm gonna lose my lunch."

"I understand, Mr. Kent, this is not what you were expecting. But I assure you the Carving Cobra C-100 makes this job much easier than any ordinary store-bought knife. It really is the only knife you'll ever need. It isn't sold in stores and it isn't even advertised. The brand relies on personal demonstration to get its names out. And I'm happy to tell you about it. Just one more cut here and . . . ah . . . .there we go." There is a slight crack and Ginsu Gary holds dead Georgie's head in his hands, smiles at the opaque, chalk white eyes. "A nice clean cut. That's what the Carving Cobra C-100 can do."

Mr. Kent winces at the sight, does his best to settle his stomach by taking another drag on his cigarette. "Dude, please, just put it in a bag or something."

Instead, Ginsu Gary places the head on the floor, where it stares at the baseboards with wild boredom. The small black cloth appears from Ginsu Gary's pocket, which he uses to wipe the blood off the blade until there is no trace it was ever used. "Would you say this is one of the most efficient knives you've ever seen, Mr. Kent?"

"What? Yeah sure. Great knife. Man, there's blood everywhere."

"Don't worry, Mr. Kent, I'll take care of that in a second. Now I ask you, how much would you expect to pay for a knife like the Carving Cobra C-100."

"Huh? Are you serious?"

Ginsu Gary turns the blade in his hand so it glimmers. "Very serious. How much would you pay? Similar retail models go for up to five hundred dollars. That's a pretty steep prince for a knife, wouldn't you say."

"No shit? Well, I guess that is a good price, considering the fucking thing just sawed through a neck bone in—"

"In two strokes. Yes, Mr. Kent, this is the knife you want, nay, the knife you'll desire, for any situation. Want to know a secret? The Carving Cobra C-100 is only ninety-nine ninety-nine. Would you say that's a fair price for this knife?"

Mr. Kent tilts his head. This creepy cleaner really likes his knife, he thinks. He checks his watch, sees it's almost 2a.m., knows he needs to get to the bosses in about thirty minutes. "Um, yeah, like I said, great price. Hey, can we hurry this up. Boss is expecting me."

"Sure, Mr. Kent. But can I show you one more thing? It'll only take a second, I promise. I can demonstrate right here on . . . George, did you say his name was."

"Whatever, yeah, just do what you gotta do. But hurry there's blood pooling around his head there and I'm two seconds away from getting sick here. "

"I understand, Mr. Kent. Now if you'll notice, the Carving Cobra C-100 also comes with a tiny hook on the end of the handle. See it?"

"Yeah. Great."

"Go ahead and hold the knife, Mr. Kent. Feel how well balanced it is in your hand." Ginsu Gary hands the knife to Mr. Kent, handle first of course. With slight confusion, Mr. Kent hefts the knife, feeling a little stupid but trying to be as accommodating as he can to the man who was sent here to dispose of his kill. Before he can comment on the knife's centre of gravity, which is admittedly quite impressive, Ginsu Gary is smiling his wide smile just inches away from his face. "Feels good in your hand, doesn't it, Mr. Kent. That's because the Carving Cobra C-100 actually was designed with ergonomic precision to eliminate wrist pain over long periods of use. Now would you say this is a knife worth its price?"

"Sure man, whatever." Mr. Kent hands the knife back. Ginsu Gary wipes the handle with his little black cloth and returns his stare to the decapitated body in the chair.

"Now what I want to show you, Mr. Kent, is just what that hook is good for. Naturally you can use it to hang the knife in your kitchen, but you've had times when you're cooking something and it's hot and you don't want to burn your hands, correct? Well watch this." Ginsu Gary grips the knife firmly, sets his jaw, and punches Georgie's stomach. The blade slips right in and his hand explodes into the organs, which sends globs of ichor all over the walls, including a few bits which add to the collection of death on Mr. Kent's suit. With a mighty yank, he pulls his hand out, along with a section of intestine that is now clasped firmly in the tiny hook on the knife.

"Hey oh, you're making more of a mess. God, I don't need to see that."

"Don't worry, Mr. Kent, I'll clean it up, it's my job. Now do you see how easy it was to get these parts out of there? Imagine if this body is on fire and you needed to get in there to grab these parts. You'd burn yourself trying to yank them out, because as you know they can be quite slippery. But with the little hook here all you have to grasp is the handle of the Carving Cobra C-100, which is made of dimpled Cherrywood, and let the hook catch its quarry. Do your knives at home have this function, Mr. Kent?"

"No they don't. I guess."

"No, I bet they don't. But the Carving Cobra C-100 does. It truly is the only knife you'll ever need."

With a gruff exhale, Mr. Kent stubs his cigarette out on the ground. "Hey no offence, Gary-whatever-your-name-is, but I don't care about the knife that much. Can we just finish this? I gotta get going. Let's just wrap him up and I'll help you get him to your trunk and you can take him wherever and finish up. As it is we're gonna need to get this blood off the floor and that's gonna take at least . . . however long that takes. I mean, you got bleach and acid and shit in there, right? We can clean this up? Like now."

"I understand, Mr. Kent, just let me finish this last demonstration and we'll move on. I think you'll be quite impressed with how fast the Carving Cobra C-

100 can complete this entire job for you. How long would you say it would normally take to dice up George here?"

"Oh Christ, I dunno, I don't care."

"Would you say it would take an hour?"

"Fucking-A dude, whatever, sure, like an hour?"

"A fair assessment, yes. Most jobs like this require an hour or more. But not with the Carving Cobra C-100. Observe." With a cock of his head, Ginsu Gary takes a little hop forward to the headless body and makes several emphatic slashes.

For a moment, Mr. Kent doesn't think the cleaner has even touched the body what with the way his swings meet no resistance. But when Ginsu Gary steps back, smiling, Mr. Kent watches the body come apart like crumbing pie crust. Hands and feet and arms and legs and torso and elbows and thighs and pelvis just slip apart from each other and collect on the floor. "See how fast that was!" exclaims Ginsu Gary. "Only the Carving Corba—"

"Fuck! Jesus, dude, that's disgusting! Ugh. And enough with the knife already. Christ what a mess. Now I'm never gonna get out of here. How are we gonna get all this blood up!"

"Not to worry, Mr. Kent, I'll take care of it. Just give me your honest thoughts on the Carving Cobra C-100. Would you say it's the only knife you'll ever need, based on what you just saw?"

Trying his best to hide his annoyance, Mr. Kent smiles through gritted teeth. "Honestly, yes, the knife is fucking amazing. Can we just—"

"Would you like to buy one?"

"What're you . . . trying to sell me knives?"

"Only if you want one. There is a special going on today for just eighty-nine ninety nine."

"Bro, no, I don't want your knife. Clean this horror show up, please! Now!"

"Can I ask why. Is it not in your budget?"

"Dude! I don't need a knife. I don't clean bodies. Get me. I don't need to cut marble and tin cans in my kitchen. I microwave hot dogs for dinner. Now I need you to clean up the massacre you just created so I can get to the Boss."

"Fair enough. Like I said, I will take care of it. Just keep thinking about that deal, I think you'll see it's a fair deal. Let me just get something out of my suit-case."

Squatting down, Ginsu Gary replaces the knife in the suitcase and begins taking out several long metallic pieces of something unknown. Like an excited child assembling Lego, he fits one piece after another to-gether, building some kind of contraption, snapping pieces in place and locking joints together. Meanwhile, Mr. Kent takes a few steps towards the couch to avoid the blooming lake of blood on the hardwood floor. When Gary stands up again, he has in fact assembled a gleaming, metallic vacuum.

"You gotta be shitting me," says Mr. Kent.

"Allow me to introduce you to the Kurbee K-10 Vacuum."

"Dude, tell me you're not gonna vacuum the rugs."

"Of course not. Not yet anyway. First let me ask you, do you have a vacuum at home?"

"Oh for the love of God, yes I do. And it works fine. But I supposes you're gonna show me how this one is better. Right? C'mon man, it's getting late."

Just then Mr. Kent's cell rings. He holds a finger up to shush the cleaner and hears Boss's voice on the other end asking him numerous questions. He does his best to keep up and give reasonable answers. "Yes, Boss. I know. Yes. I'll be there as soon as I can. I know. Yeah the cleaner is here now. A little weird? Hah! You're telling me. Weird is an understatement. The guy belongs in infommercials. No, yeah, he's fine. I'm just watching him take care of it all. Okay, I'll get outta here quick as I can." He hangs up the phone, points to the cleaner. "Boss is getting pissy. We really gotta finish up here so if you're gonna suck up hair and skin cells let's get to it, though I personally don't have any kind of record on file, so . . . "

"I understand, Mr. Kent. But before I show you what the Kurbee K-10 does, let me just ask what you would be willing to pay for a vacuum that can clean up anything off any surface. Would you be willing to pay one thousand dollars?"

"For a vacuum? Fuck no. I got a Dirt Devil and it was sixty bucks and it works great."

"Ah, but can it do this." Ginsu Gary plugs the vacuum into the wall outlet near the couch, steps on the Kurbee power switch and brings the vacuum to life.

There is barely a hum. He nods to Mr. Kent and then runs the vacuum through a glob of George's blood, sucking it up and leaving not a single drop in its wake. "Did you see how efficient that is, Mr. Kent? Now watch this." The vacuum runs over the various diced up body parts, sucking them up with a sickening crunch, but startling efficiency. The legs go schlup as they are ingested by the powerful device, the hands go grooch and are gone.

Dropping his Jaw, Mr. Kent can do nothing but stare as the cleaner runs the vacuum over every last bone, organ, and collection of gore. Wherever the vacuum goes, the body disappears, bones cracking and sinew twisting, until nothing is left but George's head, sitting by its lonesome still staring at the baseboards.

"Now what would you say if I told you the Kurbee K-10 is on sale today only for just eight hundred and fifty dollars. Would you say that's a deal?"

Mr. Kent can barely talk, entranced as he is with what he has just witnessed. "Fuck me," he says.

"Well that's one way to say it, Mr. Kent. The Kurbee K-10 sure is the bee's knees. But Mr. Kent, I repeat, what if I told you this vacuum could be yours for just eight hundred and fifty dollars. Would you say that's a deal?"

"Fuckin-A," Mr. Kent whispers, nodding at Ginsu Gary. "That's crazy."

"Of Course! Of course it is. It's a crazy good deal! Because I assure you, Mr. Kent, the Kurbee K-10 is the only model vacuum you'll ever need."

"The head," says Mr. Kent, amazed, wondering if the skull will actually fit up the vacuum.

"Yes, the head. I know what you're thinking: No way the Kurbee K-10 will pick that up. But watch this." Gary places the vacuum on the severed head and lets the machine do its work. The top of the skull cracks and the scalp peels off, whipping up into the belly of the vacuum. One eye sucks inside the skull and races out through the cranial opening to join the rest of the body in the vacuum's belly. Then the entire face caves in, gets sucked up through the open skull, before the skull itself implodes and disappears with crunching sounds into the Kurbee K-10. The blood on the floor follows until there is nothing left but lean hardwood laminate. "Pretty impressive, huh, Mr. Kent. "

Kent stares in disbelief, dumbstruck, and somehow invigorated by the show. "That's the hell of a machine, man. How in the world does it work?"

"The Kurbee K-10 is all handmade, Mr. Kent, and comes with a two year warranty. Now I ask you, would you be willing to pay eight hundred and fifty dollars for this kind of craftsmanship?"

"I suppose I would. I mean, if I was in need of a vacuum cleaner to do...that."

"Tell you what, Mr. Kent, for this one time deal, I can drop an additional twenty five dollars if you're interested."

"I don't really need a new vacuum."

Ginsu Gary motions for Mr. Kent to try the machine, ultimately placing the handle in his hands. "Go ahead, just give it a push. It doesn't bite."

After a few pushes, Mr. Kent gives the handle back to the cleaner. "It moves well, sure. But hey, now that this is done, weirder than I could have fucking imagined, I gotta get to the Boss. Are we good here?"

"Well, that depends. I'd like to show you how the Kurbee K-10 can even wash windows. If you'll follow me to the windows over here—"

"Look, honestly, I don't need any more demonstrations, the vacuum is a killer machine. I get it."

"So what do you say, can I put you down for one?" Ginsu Gary stares at Mr. Kent with a toothy grin and bright eyes, refusing to break contact. "It's the best deal in town. You should really get one. And tell you what. I'll throw in the Carving Cobra C-100 for only forty dollars. Now would you say that's a deal? Say yes and I can get it set up right now. I've got one of each in my suitcase just looking for a new home. What do you say? Only eight hundred and sixty five dollars."

It's obvious the cleaner is going to keep hounding Mr. Kent about selling his wares. And in any other normal situation Kent would have told the guy to fuck off and shoved him away. But no use upsetting the Boss anymore. And it is hard to deny the astounding capabilities of both products. He pats his jacket's inner pocket and knows he's carry at least three grand in cash. Always cash. Never credit cards or checks. Nothing to connect him to the grid. Even his driver's license is a fake, which is how the Boss prefers his strong arms to be. Ginsu Gary edges closer, slowly nodding his head as if to make the decision for him. There is something stubborn in his nod, the way it is steady and unwavering. Finally Kent relents and pulls out his wad of cash. "You know, Boss said you were weird and I gotta agree, but considering what I just saw is still blowing my mind, yeah, I'll take your deal."

"Perfect!" Ginsu Gary claps his hands, moves to his suitcase and removes the parts for the vacuum as well as the knife. How it all fits in there is a mystery to Mr. Kent. Ginsu Gary hands a brand new knife to Mr. Kent then quickly assembles the vacuum cleaner. "Mr. Kent, I thank you for your business. You won't regret this."

As Mr. Kent studies the knife's blade in his hands, the cleaner packs up his stuff, heads to the door, and turns back once to say, "Have a good night, Mr. Kent." With that, he opens the door and leaves.

"Weirdo," Mr. Kent whispers, looking at his new vacuum and the room before him. Not a single bit of evidence betrays the fact that a murder and bodily dismemberment ever took place here. Quite the damn machine, he thinks, wondering just what he will try to vacuum with it first. Perhaps his annoying neighbor's teenage son who plays his shitty rap music so loud every night. He checks his watch, realizes he is beyond late now, grabs his new Kurbee K-10, and heads for the door as well. Before he can open it a man enters and stands before him.

"Who the hell are you?" Kent asks, feeling the weight of his gun in his shoulder holster.

The man is wearing black rubber gloves and dark sunglasses, carrying a suitcase and a tarp. A mild facial tic makes his nose twitch like a mouse and he squints creepily. "Boss said you had a body here. I'm the cleaner. Sorry I'm late, there was an accident on the highway. You can leave though, I'll take care of it. Boss told me you need to get back to the office, so I'll just grab the body and go. Where is it? Hey, you hear me? Are you okay? You look confused. What's wrong with you? And why are you holding a knife and a vacuum?"

ABOUT THE AUTHOR

Ryan C. Thomas is an award-winning journalist, author, and musician living in San Diego. You can usually find him in the bars on the weekends playing guitar. When he's not writing or rocking out, he's either reading comics or watching really cheesy movies. Visit him on-line at www.ryancthomas.com

NOVELS:
The Summer I Died
Born To Bleed
Salticidae
Hissers
Hissers 2: Death March
The Undead World of Oz
Ratings Game

NOVELLAS:
With a Face of Golden Pleasure
Enemy Unseen
Choose
The Scent of Fear

COLLECTIONS:
Scraps & Chum

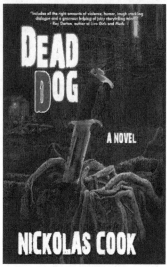

ISBN: 978-1937727246

DEAD DOG

BY NICKOLAS COOK

It's the late 70s and Max and Little Billy are back from Vietnam trying to mind their own business when they stumble onto the murder of a local boy. With organized crime and local thugs on their trail, it's up to these two heroes to solve the murder.

WALKING SHADOW
by Clifford Royal Johns

ISBN: 9781937727253

Benny tries to ignore the payment-overdue messages he keeps getting from "Forget What?," a memory removal company. Benny's a slacker, after all, and couldn't pay them even if he wanted to. Then people start trying to kill him, and his life suddenly depends on finding out what memories he has forgotten. Benny relies on his wits, latent skills, and new friends as he investigates his own past; delving deeper and deeper into the underworld of criminals, bad cops, and shady news organizations, all with their own reasons for wanting him to remain ignorant or die.

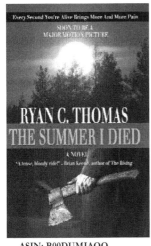

For more Grand Mal Press titles
please visit us online at
www.grandmalpress.com

28754778R10145

Made in the USA
San Bernardino, CA
07 January 2016